D0966528

GOTCHA!

INSIDE TRUMP'S 2020 CAMPAIGN

A NOVEL BY

ED. WEINBERGER

Copyright © 2020 by Ed. Weinberger

All rights reserved.

No part of this publication in print or in electronic format may be reproduced, stored in a retrieval system, or transmitted in any form or by any means, electronic, mechanical, photocopying, recording, or otherwise without the prior written permission of the publisher.

This is a work of fiction. Names, characters, organizations, places, events and incidents are either the products of the author's imagination or are used fictitiously. Any resemblance to actual persons, living or dead, or actual events is purely coincidental.

eBook ISBN: 978-1-64704-246-2
Paperback ISBN: 978-1-64704-233-2
Hardcover ISBN: 978-1-64704-245-5

Cover illustration by Hashim Lafond

In memory of Dick Gregory

1932 — 2017

Author's Note

This book — a product of the author's imagination — is a work of satirical fiction. Its parodies and exaggerated distortions are solely intended for the reader's amusement. Those seeking moral instruction should look elsewhere.

'Tis strange — but true, for truth is always strange: Stranger than fiction, if it could be told. How much would novels gain by the advantage!

Lord Byron — from the satirical poem Don Juan, 1823

CONTENTS

CHAPTER 1

ELECTION DAY: NOVEMBER 3, 2020 — MAR-A-LAGO

Daybreak.

Donald Trump opened the lid of his Da Vinci TheraLight 360 tanning bed ($85,000 retail), stepped out, and plodded — naked — into his clothes closet.

He dressed for the day in Palm Beach casual: white flannel slacks, white sports shirt open at the neck, white Christian Louboutin loafers with the dandelion tassel and three-inch lifts. His navy blue blazer with gold buttons had the Trump coat of arms on the right breast pocket. In front of the full-length mirror behind the closet door, he posed for himself. Not a care in the world for a man $500 million in debt.

The view from the Mar-a-Lago master bedroom was all ocean. All the way to the horizon — a dark blue, almost purple, not unlike the color Trump chose for the bedroom walls in the high-roller suites of his Atlantic City Taj Mahal.

Now and then you could spot a Coast Guard patrol boat, silently darting back and forth, beyond the soundproof glass. All else was monotonous sea and dull sky.

But Donald Trump's gaze was fixed instead on the three Samsung flat screens catty-corner from his California King. One was tuned to *Fox & Friends First*; the second to CNN's *New Day*; and the third to *Morning Joe*, where Joe Scarborough had just giddily announced that Vegas had listed Trump a 5-2 underdog to Joe Biden.

Just because Trump had said Scarborough "murdered a young female intern" didn't mean Trump didn't watch his show.

In October 2019, Trump officially left New York City and recorded a Declaration of Domicile in Palm Beach County, where there was no state tax and no federal prosecutors from the Southern District. And so it would be here, at his private residence at The Mar-a-Lago Club, that he would watch the election returns with selected family members and Senior Advisers.

Mar-a-Lago was built from 1924 to 1927, for around $90 million in today's money, by Marjorie Merriweather Post, heiress to the Post Cereal fortune. The mansion had fifty-eight bedrooms, thirty-three bathrooms, twelve fireplaces, and three bomb shelters.

When she died in 1973, the estate couldn't give the place away. After sitting empty for more than ten years, Trump purchased the abandoned property in 1985 for around $10 million, including the furniture.

Along with the mansion, furniture, and its seventeen acres, Trump acquired a coat of arms, which had been granted to Marjorie Post's third husband by the British Royal Family. It featured three lions surrounding a pair of chevrons, with an outstretched arm holding an arrow. The text at the bottom read "Integritas" ("integrity" for those with little

Latin). Not surprisingly, Trump — without permission — removed the word "integritas" and replaced it with the word "Trump."

And it is that coat of arms that today is not only displayed on Trump's blazer, but flies under the American flag from the 80-foot pole on the grounds of Mar-a-Lago.

Over the years, Trump had personally supervised the mansion's extensive remodeling. He'd built a separate, closed-off area and grounds for him and his family. He added a 20,000-square-foot ballroom (large enough to entertain 800 guests) and spent $100,000 on four gold-plated sinks in the women's bathrooms.

In the drawing room — modeled on a Venetian palace — he hung a six-foot oil painting of himself wearing a tennis sweater. Trump labeled his portrait, "The Visionary."

In 1995, Trump turned Mar-a-Lago into a private club and, after becoming President, built a communications facility with a White House-style Situation Room where, in February 2017, he ordered a Tomahawk missile strike on a Syrian airfield before having dinner with his guests at the time, Chinese President Xi Jinping and his wife.

The bombing was soon the talk of the table.

Membership at Mar-a-Lago costs $200,000 (with dues coming to around $20,000 per year), and there's a three-year waiting list despite the seventy-eight health violations, including those for unsafe seafood, rusty shelving, cooks without hairnets, and smoked salmon "served without proper destruction of parasites."

Mar-a-Lago is also where a 16-year-old locker room attendant (Virginia Roberts) was recruited by Ghislaine Maxwell to service the multimillionaire club member Jeffrey Epstein.

8:00 a.m.

Trump — hair coiffed and gelled — strode down the corridor to the family room where he would watch the returns. A Secret

Service agent, posted nearby, whispered into his lapel: "'Mogul' (the Secret Service code name for the President; Melania's was 'Muse') is on the move."

The 3,000-square-foot family room had been arranged like a movie theater, with plush leather chairs facing a wall of TV screens. At the far end, uniformed waiters from Mar-a-Lago's Palm Garden Room set up a breakfast buffet: sliced melons, cantaloupe, and honeydew. Assorted fruit-flavored yogurts. Sides of bacon, maple sausage, and home-fried potatoes. Entrees of buttermilk pancakes. French toast and Belgian waffles. Stationed behind a cooktop, a chef in a white toque prepared the fixings for "two eggs cooked your way." Eggs Benedict. Omelets with choice of toppings. A young Hispanic waitress put out cups and saucers for tea, espresso, cappuccino, coffee, and decaf.

Trump, who as a rule skipped breakfast (there were some days Trump could go twelve to fourteen hours without food), had already gobbled two McDonald's Egg McMuffins microwaved in the Mar-a-Lago kitchen. He considered it his lucky breakfast. It was the same breakfast he had eaten four years ago at his New York condo in Trump Tower — the day he had been elected President of the United States in a spectacular upset that surprised the world and even Trump himself — though he was not likely to admit it.

9:15 a.m.

The six 75-inch TV screens — each showing a different network — were flooded with images of Trump surrogates making their last-minute appeals to the voters — among them, Corey Lewandowski, Press Secretary Kayleigh McEnany, South Carolina Senator Tim Scott, Senator of Arkansas Tom Cotton, and Governor Ron DeSantis of Florida. At the same time, a vast communications team led by the trusted Hope Hicks was calling Top-5 radio shows in key markets such as Ohio, Pennsylvania, and Florida.

Between phone calls to pals like Chris Christie and billionaire Carl Icahn, Trump watched the TVs — remote in hand — switching rapidly from one station to the next.

The family room was filling up. Hope Hicks was the first to arrive, followed by Trump's son Eric and wife Lara; Don Jr. and his girlfriend Kimberly Guilfoyle, the former Fox News personality and now National Chair of the Trump Victory Finance Committee; and — alone — Tiffany Trump, Marla Maples' daughter, who had been given a broom closet of a room in the main building.

Jared and Ivanka, having voted in New York earlier that morning, were on their way down on the family jet and were expected to arrive by lunch.

The previous Saturday (October 31, 2020), Ivanka — as superstitious as her father — and Jared (both Orthodox Jews) had made a conspicuous visit to a Queens synagogue to say their prayers and pay their respects at the Ohel (literally, a tent; in this case, a tomb) — the resting place of the beloved, world-renowned Rebbe Menachem Mendel Schneerson, just as they had done four years ago on the Saturday before Trump's election.

There would be no children here today. Trump had always been uncomfortable around children, especially when they were his own.

Nor could you expect to see Vice President Mike Pence and his wife Karen. Pence, his staff, and the bulk of Trump supporters and campaign workers were being housed seventy-five miles away — at Trump's International Doral Hotel and Golf Club where, as a comedian once put it, "the mosquitos are so big, after they take your blood they hand out coffee and donuts."

11:10 a.m.

The first votes in the nation were tallied in the small town of Dixville, New Hampshire — population 15. The vote count was Trump 5, Biden 5. As Katy Tur of MSNBC noted, the vote might very well be a forecast of the day to come. That is, a close, very close election.

Over at CNN, however, commentators John King, Wolf Blitzer, and Jake Tapper were predicting an easy Biden victory based on early exit polls. "Same thing they said four years ago," scoffed Trump.

Trump was still buoyed from last night's rally — the final stop of the campaign — held in Orlando's Amway Arena before a crowd of ten thousand rabid supporters. The eighty-minute speech was half TelePrompter, half ad-lib, and his raucous fans enjoyed every minute of it, interrupting with chants of "Four More Years!" and "USA!"

They especially loved the new one he had added a couple of rallies ago: "And who's going to pay for the virus?" he'd yell. "China!" came the answer, roaring back at him.

To those who had been following his campaign with a rooting interest, the speech hit all the right notes: the fake news and Media Liars. The unhinged Mobs marching in the streets. Antifa coming for your guns. Your houses. Your women. Dire predictions of widespread voter fraud. And his perfect economy until ruined by the onslaught of the virus with many names, like the Yellow Peril and the Kung-Flu. Or his personal favorite — the Jinx from the Chinks.

Trump was especially pleased with his imitation of Biden as a tottering old man. He had thought of it on the spot — an improvised five minutes that had his audience screaming with laughter. He had always marveled at his ability to say or do whatever came to mind, without giving it a second thought.

Besides the good-sized crowd — maybe the best of the campaign — the Fox numbers were better than usual, drawing over 4.6 million viewers. In addition, his vendors had sold more than $35,000 in merchandising: MAGA hats, T-shirts, and even some "Clinton rape whistles" left over from 2016.

Trump's good mood quickly spread, lightening the always-present tension whenever he was near. Laughs shifted from chair to chair above the clatter.

Two weeks ago, the polls showed him trailing by eight to ten points nationally. But the race tightened considerably, especially after he said he wasn't going to pay pollsters who had him losing.

And, in the last month, a couple of gaffes by Joe Biden had only helped — thanking the NAACP for its endorsement, Biden called it the NCAA. Worse, during a live TV talk with Obama, Biden had referred to the former President as Barack bin Laden.

12:05 p.m.

Melania appeared, like a burst of sunlight, in a sleeveless yellow silk Azzedine Alaïa midi-dress (retail price $6,500), her #10 Cartier Paris 18k gold sunglasses (retail price $25,000) perched perfectly on top of her just-done hair.

She silently made her stately way to the yogurt station — her sunglasses never moved an inch. Little known was the fact that Melania had as much at stake in the outcome of today's election as her husband. Maybe even more so.

According to the latest rumors, her lawyers had just finished negotiating a new prenup that guaranteed her $50 million if she stayed in the White House four more years, with an extra $75,000 in bonuses per every Christmas tree lighting, Easter egg hunt, and July 4th celebration.

With cappuccino in hand, she took a seat three rows behind her husband. Over the years, Melania and Trump had developed more of a brother-and-sister relationship. Which one was the brother and which one was the sister, however, was not always discernible.

"Who's winning?" Melania asked huskily to no one in particular.

* * *

CHAPTER 2

EIGHT MONTHS EARLIER — THE COMMITTEE TO REELECT

For most students of the Trump White House, the campaign to reelect the President began on his Inauguration Day. Everything done in the four years of his presidency since — every decision, every speech, every law signed, every deregulation, every photo op, every round-table conference — was calculated to ensure a second term in 2020.

For the record, however, we can set the official date as March 5, 2020 when Trump's most trusted inner circle met in the White House — in the Roosevelt Room in the West Wing, a short walk from the Oval Office — as a select committee to plot the strategies for the coming campaign to reelect the President.

The Roosevelt Room has an honored place in American history. On December 7, 1941, it was in this room that Secretary of State Cordell

Hull had kept three diplomats from Tokyo waiting while down the hall he and President Roosevelt listened to the reports from Hawaii that the Japanese had just bombed Pearl Harbor.

In 1969, Richard Nixon officially named the room after both Teddy Roosevelt, who first built the West Wing, and his second cousin Franklin, who had expanded it into its present space.

It is a windowless room — perfect for important conferences and presentations. On its Georgian-yellow walls hang portraits of Franklin, seated, and Teddy on horseback. Centered on the east wall is a never-lit fireplace.

Except for bottles of Trump water, the long conference table was bare: no computers, yellow legal pads, or cell phones. This was a meeting that would appear on no one's calendar.

It was the first meeting of CRET — the Committee to ReElect Trump — as they called themselves. Anti-Trumpers added "In

November" to the acronym so the word became CRETIN.

There were twelve of them — their faces stern and somber, befitting of men and women about to wage war for the soul of America. Those who were there that day were:

BRAD PARSCALE

Campaign Manager. Digital guru credited for Trump's 2016 victory. Campaign Portfolio: Online Fundraising. Digital Advertising. Trump's Facebook page. Data Science. And Polling. To date, companies owned by Parscale had been paid over $40 million from the President's various reelection committees. From those funds, Parscale and his wife Candice purchased for themselves a Ferrari, a Range Rover, a $400,000 boat, two $1 million condos, and a $2.4 million waterfront house in Ft. Lauderdale, Florida. News of those purchases caused a temporary riff between Parscale and Trump, which was soon patched up.

JARED KUSHNER

Senior Adviser and son-in-law. Official White House title: "Director of the Office of American Innovation." Tasked in 2016 by the President to bring peace to the Middle East. Campaign Portfolio: Digital Media. Fundraising. Strategy. Orthodox Jew who observes the Jewish sabbath (Friday sundown to Saturday sundown), even in the White House.

In 2004, Kushner's father was indicted on eighteen felony counts for tax fraud and witness tampering, including hiring a prostitute in an attempt to blackmail his brother-in-law. In 2015, Kushner and his two brothers founded a real estate platform and were given a $250 million line of credit by billionaire George Soros, Democratic donor.

In 2019, the Maryland Attorney General filed a complaint accusing Kushner's real estate complexes of failing to take action on thousands of apartments with rodent infestations and forcing tenants (mostly black and brown occupants) to pay illegitimate fees. Kushner was also labeled a "Tier-One Predator" in a Netflix documentary titled *Slumlord Millionaire.*

IVANKA TRUMP

Senior Adviser to the President and First Daughter. The first Jewish daughter of the First Family, having converted before marrying Jared Kushner in 2009. Her Hebrew name is "Yael" ("desert-dwelling goat"). Keeps Kosher and like her husband observes the Jewish Sabbath. The boyfriend she dated before Kushner was also Jewish: Bingo Gubelman, rich playboy and TV producer later arrested in a cocaine bust.

In 2016, Ivanka won a Fashion Industry Award in the Accessory division. Later that year, the U.S. Consumer Safety Commission ordered the recall of all her scarves (made in China) because of their high level of flammability. Campaign Portfolio: Strategy and Event Planning. She was also Trump's first choice for Vice President until cooler heads prevailed.

KELLYANNE CONWAY

Senior Adviser. Longtime Trump advocate. Graduated with Honors from George Washington Law School. Grandfather was Jimmy "The Brute" DiNatale, once a mob associate of a Philadelphia crime family. First met Trump when she and her husband purchased a condo in Trump Tower. Campaign Portfolio: Communications Director and Spin Doctor. Husband is George Conway III, attorney and conservative Republican, who has publicly called Trump "unfit for office." *(Author's note: Kellyanne Conway would not finish the campaign. She announced on August 23, 2020 she'd be leaving her position as Senior Adviser to the President to "focus on her family." At least that's the story she gave at the time.)*

ROBERT JEFFRIES

Religious adviser. Often called "Trump's Apostle." Pastor of the First Baptist Church in Dallas, Texas (members: 15,000). Author of twenty-seven books, including *Countdown to the*

Apocalypse and *When It's Okay* Not *to Forgive*. Called Obama the anti-Christ for his support of same-sex marriage. Suggested that Islam promotes pedophilia, and, during the 2019 impeachment of Trump by Congress, said that if the Democrats were successful, it would cause a "civil war fracture in this nation."

HOPE HICKS

Counselor to the President. Campaign Portfolio: Communications. Scheduling. Gatekeeper to the President. Former teenage model. Joined Trump Organization in 2014 as assistant to Ivanka. Rewarded for her work as Press Secretary in the 2016 campaign with a White House job as Communications Director. Resigned from the White House in 2018 to join Fox News as Head of Public Relations. Returned to the White House in February 2020 as aide to Jared Kushner and Counselor to Donald Trump. Her reasons for leaving, and reasons for returning, remain unknown.

Linked romantically in 2016 to Campaign Manager Corey Lewandowski — then married with four children.

COREY LEWANDOWSKI

Trump's first Campaign Manager in 2016 before being replaced by now-convicted felon Paul Manafort. Presently back in Trump's good graces as co-Campaign Manager working out of Arlington, Virginia headquarters. Campaign Portfolio: Ground Game. Event Planner. Reportedly fired in 2016 for failure to moderate his taste for hard liquor.

RALPH REED

Religious Consultant. Best known as the founder of the Christian Coalition (1990s). Currently Chairman of the Georgia Republican Party and CEO of the Family and Freedom Coalition.

Campaign Portfolio: getting out the vote of 35 million Evangelicals. A born-again Christian who came to the Lord when visited by the Holy

Spirit while drinking in a Washington, D.C. bar called Bullfeathers.

STEPHEN MILLER

Senior Adviser. Campaign Portfolio: Speech Writer. Immigration Policy. Miller was once Press Secretary for Michele Bachmann, Congresswoman from Minnesota who called Obama an anti-American foreigner and accused Hillary Clinton's State Department aide Huma Abedin of being a member of the Muslim Brotherhood.

Grandson of Russian immigrants, Miller was born Jewish but is nonobservant. His leaked emails from 2019 reveal curious sympathies with ultra-right activists and their publications. Miller is chief architect of Trump's anti-immigration policies, which have been summed up by the question: "Why not more Norwegians?" Married to Katie Waldman, Press Secretary to Mike Pence, Waldman is a strong supporter of her husband's programs, especially those separating migrant children from their parents.

LEV BECKERMAN

Shadowy, mysterious political operative. Newest and least-known member of Trump's election committee. Former Colonel in charge of covert operations for Mossad, Israel's secret intelligence organization. Recommended to Jared Kushner by Benjamin Netanyahu, Israeli Prime Minister. Campaign Portfolio: Opposition Research. Misinformation. Cyber Security. Worked on the campaigns of (and helped elect) Madagascar's right-wing President Andry Bajoelina, Hungarian dictator Viktor Orbán, and Fascist President of Brazil Jair Bolsonaro.

DONALD TRUMP JR.

Eldest child of Donald Trump. Executive Vice President of the Trump Organization. Campaign Portfolio: Fundraising. Surrogate. Liaison to NRA. Famous for retweeting conspiracy theories of the right-wing white supremacists such as Alex Jones, Kevin B. MacDonald, and James Edwards — including the anti-Semitic theory that Democratic donor George Soros turned fellow Jews into the Nazis during World War II. An avid hunter, Donald Jr. was once pictured with a knife in one hand and a bloody elephant tail in the other.

JAY SEKULOW

Lawyer for the President. Called God's smartest lawyer, Sekulow has argued and won some of the most high-profile cases on behalf of the religious right in the last decade. Campaign Portfolio: All things "Legal." A former Jew, he converted to Christianity when — in a debate with a college roommate — Sekulow could not think of any reasons why Jesus was not the true Messiah.

It would appear on the surface that all those present were uniform in their desire to reelect the President. In truth, each harbored his or her own secret (and not-too-secret) agenda. And, as well, a distrust of (if not hostility toward) some of their fellow compatriots.

There were the opportunists and the ideologues. The moderates and the hard-right wingers. There were the Jews, the non-Jews, the former Jews, and the anti-Semites.

That these fissures would appear in the course of the coming campaign was a given; how deep and wide the cracks would become is another story.

At exactly 1:30 p.m., Parscale called the meeting to order, then asked Pastor Jeffries to give the opening prayer. Members bowed their heads and joined hands:

PASTOR JEFFRIES

Heavenly Father, we assemble here today that your Holy Spirit may bless us, our nation, and our President — Donald Trump. May you secure our President in your Heavenly spirit as he continues on the path of righteousness, as he continues his quest to make God great in America again. Please, Lord — release Your wisdom upon the men and women gathered here today so they will have the strength, the courage, and the grace to advise our President so that, as the Bible says, Your will be done here on Earth as it is in Heaven. In Jesus' name, Amen.

After the "Amens," Parscale called everyone's attention to the PowerPoint presentation: slides that showed the ten major issues of the Trump campaign for 2020. They were, in reverse order of importance:

10. Israel
    * Israel's best friend is Trump
    * Done more for Israel than any President since Truman
    * Voting Targets: Broward and Dade Counties, Florida; suburban Philadelphia; Evangelicals

9. Criminal Justice
    * Prison reform

* Nonviolent offenders given a second chance
* Special Targets: black and Hispanic voters

8. Religious Freedom
    * End attacks on Christianity and its churches
    * End separation of Church and State
    * Special Targets: Evangelicals

7. Gun Laws
    * Protect the Second Amendment
    * Extend gun laws to every state, i.e., "stand your ground" and "open carry"
    * Special Targets: Colorado, Wyoming, Nevada, Arizona, Georgia, Florida, Michigan

6. Supreme Court
    * Maintain conservative majority
    * Appoint Originalists to Court
    * All judges approved by Federalist Society

5. Abortion
    * End Roe v. Wade
    * National ban on all abortions after two weeks
    * Special Targets: Catholic Democrats, the Base

4. Voter Protection
    * Voter ID laws
    * Protect democracy
    * Vote-by-mail fraud
    * Special Target: the Base

3. Immigration
    * Finish the wall
    * Define and defend our borders
    * Close our borders
    * Special Target: the Base

2. The Economy
    * Steady job growth
    * Lowest unemployment (among African Americans)
    * Surging stock market
    * New trade deals with China (billions for America)
    * Special Targets: African Americans, lower-income whites, workers with 401(k)s

1. Joe Biden
    * Corrupt ties to China and Ukraine
    * Onset dementia
    * Plagiarism
    * "Sleepy Joe"

The last slide contained one sentence: "IDENTITY POLITICS IS THE NAME OF THE GAME."

There was confidence in the air as they adjourned. The economy couldn't be better. The stock market was riding high. And they were sitting on a war chest of over $350 million — $15 million of which was already targeted for ads attacking the vulnerable Joe Biden. And so back to work they went, many to the West Wing, happily unaware that at this very moment, there was a distant virus slinking its ugly way in their direction.

* * *

CHAPTER 3

LAURA INGRAHAM COMES TO THE WHITE HOUSE

Laura Ingraham, Fox News anchor, had a dinner date with the President. The meeting had been set up by her colleague Sean Hannity — not that Ingraham, with a TV audience of 3.9 million viewers a night — didn't have the clout to call the President directly, but Hannity had easier access and Ingraham wanted to make sure that the President knew she had critical information that needed to be shared personally.

The date was March 6 and the United States, at the time, had reported 332 cases of the coronavirus with the number of deaths listed at 17. But Ingraham, attuned to the public's growing fears about the virus, was acutely aware that the President was about to face a serious PR problem that could very well hinder his chances for reelection eight months later. In other words, the President needed help and she was ready and able to provide it.

At first, she had hoped for, at best, a quick meeting in the Oval Office, but it was Trump — intrigued by what he had heard from Hannity — who suggested he and Ingraham meet alone for dinner in the President's dining room.

The President's private dining room is located in the northwest corner on the second floor, overlooking the North Lawn. It was in 1961 that Jacqueline Kennedy transformed what was then called the Lincoln Bedroom into the President's dining room. Since then, it had gone through extensive remodeling. Each administration adding and altering the décor, carpeting, and wallpaper.

Today, the room is furnished in Federal-style antiques. Sheraton-style chairs surround a Sheraton-style pedestal table. Trump's own touches included the gold-hued curtains, the orangey rug with a leaf pattern, and a cream-colored, subtly printed wallpaper. He also had the chairs reupholstered in a gold brocade to match the drapes.

The dinner was arranged for 6:00 p.m. The President liked to dine early; Ingraham had arrived at 5:40 and was sitting at the table in front of one of the two place settings, waiting patiently, when the President arrived right on time — looking like he had just stepped fresh from the shower.

What follows is the exact transcript of that dinner between Laura Ingraham and President Donald J. Trump:

The President: *(entering)* I hope you like meat loaf.

Ingraham: Love it. Yum. Comfort food. My favorite.

The President: And jumbo shrimp cocktail.

Ingraham: You read my mind, Mr. President.

Benjamin, an African American butler, enters with a pitcher of water.

Benjamin: Anything to drink, sir?

The President: My usual Diet Coke, Benjamin. Laura?

Ingraham: Diet Coke will be perfect, thank you.

Benjamin exits.

The President: That's Benjamin. He's been here forever. First, I thought Obama hired him, so I fired him right off. Then they told me he's been here since Reagan, so I hired him back. He's got the perfect look for a butler, don't you think? Black with white hair. Right out of Central Casting.

Ingraham: You know, Mr. President, you probably don't remember this, but back in the day — your bachelor days — we actually went out on a date.

The President: No kidding?

Ingraham: I know you won't remember, but you took me to dinner at, I think it was called The Quilted Giraffe...

The President: Oh yeah, on Second Avenue somewhere.

Ingraham: You were driving this big Cadillac with the personalized license plate 'DJT'.

The President: That was way before anybody else had them. I was the first.

Ingraham: And you never called me again.

The President: I like women with breasts. Maybe that was it. *(Pause)*

Have you ever thought of implants? That'd lift your ratings at least 25%.

(Author's note: After Laura Ingraham's date with Donald Trump, she told a girlfriend he was so vain, all he talked about was himself. "He needed two cars," she had said, "one for him and another for his hair." Many years later, Trump had commented about Laura Ingraham that "she was the only blonde at Fox News that Roger Ailes didn't try to fuck.")

Pause.

The President: You sure you wouldn't like some French wine? They got great French wine here. They even have a couple bottles that Thomas Jefferson brought over from Paris.

Ingraham: No, thank you, Mr. President. I'm afraid I'm a 100% teetotaler.

The President: So am I. As you've probably heard.

Ingraham: When I saw what alcohol did to my father, I never wanted to go near the stuff.

The President: That was the way it was with my older brother. Terrible drunk. He was working for Pan Am as a pilot and one day he flew from New York to Chicago and when he landed he told the passengers 'Welcome to St. Louis.' They fired him the next day. Never flew again. Washed up at 40.

Ingraham: One night they found my father — drunk — in the middle of a barbershop. He told the police he had broken in because he wanted to give himself a haircut.

Benjamin enters, bringing them their shrimp cocktails and Diet Cokes.

The President: *(eating)* Terrible thing *(INAUDIBLE)...*

Ingraham: I hate to admit it, but my father was also a bit of a Nazi sympathizer. Ten beers and he'd be marching through the house singing 'Deutschland Über Alles'.

The President: You don't say. You know, my grandfather was from Germany, which is probably why my father joined the Bund. *(Author's note: American organization known as Friends of the New Germany.)* Of course, that was way before D-Day. *(beat)* He used to carry this picture in his wallet of a Hitler Youth girl, in boots, riding pants, and naked from the waist up. Every once in a while, for no reason, he'd just take it out and show it around. After the war started, he told everybody we were Swedish.

Pause.

Ingraham: These days, if you say one nice thing about Hitler, they send the PC Police after you.

The President: Political correctness. Very terrible. You take me, for example. After that march in Charlottesville...

Ingraham: Oh, I remember.

The President: And that group — what were they called?

Ingraham: Unite the Right.

The President: That's them. And I said there were good people on both sides. And suddenly I'm anti-Semitic. I'm the least anti-Semitic person in the world...

Ingraham: I understand completely. They call me homophobic.

The President: I didn't know that.

Ingraham: Oh yes. Even my own brother called me a homophobic monster.

The President: Why would he say a thing like that?

Ingraham: Because he's a flaming fag. That's why.

The President: Well, I'm the least anti-Semitic person who ever lived. I love Jewish people. All my lawyers are Jewish. All my accountants are Jewish. Some of my biggest donors are Jewish. Adelson, Singer, Ichan — a Jew with money are some of the best people in the world...

Ingraham: They are clever. I got to give them that much.

The President: Well, they're not all that smart. I went to Fordham with this Jew named Joe Shapiro. Wanted to transfer to an Ivy League school, so he asked me to take his SATs for him.

Ingraham: Did you?

The President: I wanted to be a nice guy so sure. *(beat)* He not only got into Yale, but they gave him a full scholarship. *(pause)* I see by your cross you're Christian.

Ingraham: I was raised Baptist, but I converted to Catholicism.

The President: I can see that. Baptists — you gotta sing, you gotta dance, you gotta confess in public. Catholics — all you have to do is sit and kneel.

Ingraham: Catholicism saved my life.

The President: Good for you.

Ingraham: That's when I found Jesus. Finally, I met a man I could trust.

The President: Great person Jesus. Doesn't get half the credit he deserves...

Benjamin enters. Clears the shrimp cocktails and sets down the meat loaf and a bottle of ketchup.

The President: *(casually)* Hannity mentioned you wanted to talk to me about this Chinese virus that's going around?

Ingraham: Clearly, the Democrats think they can use it against you.

The President: I know. Another hoax. First the Russian hoax. Then the Ukrainian hoax. Now it's the coronavirus hoax. Nothing but Fake News.

Ingraham: Hard to believe they think they can turn a simple flu into this... this pandemic.

The President: Heart disease kills more people in a year.

Ingraham: More people die in swimming pools than are going to die from the virus.

The President: And those who are going to die — not that even one death is something I'm in favor of — are half dead already.

Ingraham: No question — they're inflating the numbers to make you look bad. Every time they announce a death from COVID, the faces over on MSNBC light up like kids on Christmas morning.

The President: Well, we got it under control. Nothing to worry about.

Ingraham: But these stay-at-home orders from those Democratic governors are destroying your economy.

The President: Greatest economy in history. Stock market breaking records. Unemployment lower than it's ever been. Then — this Chinese hoax comes along...

Ingraham: That's what worries me, Mr. President. Especially with people around you like this Dr. Fauci telling everybody to stay at home. And talking like it's the end of the world. I mean, give me a break.

The President: I know. They got these what... these 'models' that say 60,000 dead in six months? Something like that anyway.

Ingraham: And worse, they're making it sound like it's all your fault.

The President: I'm not worried. Because come summer, maybe spring even, it's all going to disappear. Like it was never here.

Ingraham: In the meantime, I think I have something that could totally be a game changer.

The President: What kind of game changer?

Ingraham: Friends of mine in Silicon Valley have tipped me off to a possible cure for the coronavirus. It's called hydroxychloroquine.

The President: Hydro—

Ingraham: *(slowly)* Hy-drox-y-chlor-o-quine.

The President: Hydroxychloroquine.

Ingraham: You've got it. And from my sources, it could be not only effective in treating COVID-19 but cure it.

The President: What kind of sources?

Ingraham: Elon Musk for one. Two doctors at Stanford Medical

School — James Todaro and Gregory Rigano. And besides them, there's a paper written by a French researcher who's actually tried the drug on COVID patients and it cured them. His name is Dr. Didier Raoult, he's been using a combination of hydroxychloroquine and the anti-bacterial medication Azithromycin — in a sort of Z-Pak. *(pause)* I'm breaking the news on my show next week and I wanted to let you know about it first.

The President: And you say it works?

Ingraham: I'm convinced. According to these Stanford doctors, it will get rid of the virus completely.

The President: Who makes it?

Ingraham: A French company called Sanofi.

The President: Sanofi? That's publicly traded?

Ingraham: Yeah, and there's a hedge company called Dodge & Cox that's heavily invested in it.

The President: Bet the stock'll take off like gang busters when you do your story...

Pause.

Ingraham: Even more important — it could single-handedly bring back the economy. And it's perfectly safe. It's been on the market for thirty years. People have been taking it since the Fifties — for malaria and lupus. Of course, you might have to get the FDA to approve it for COVID...

The President: Not a problem. If it's all you say it is, what with people dying, what have they got to lose?

Ingraham: *(confidentially)* Mr. President, I've heard that right now there are hospitals in New York where doctors and nurses are taking it as a preventative...

The President: Right now?

Ingraham: Yes sir. Right now.

The President: And who knows about this besides you, the researchers, and Musk?

Ingraham: You, me, and Dr. Oz.

Long pause.

The President: Laura, got to hand it to you. This is a game changer.

Ingraham: I know! And the last thing the Dems want to hear. That the President they've hated from the day you took office has come up with a cure for the coronavirus that they're predicting will bring America to its knees.

Benjamin enters with apple pie and vanilla ice cream for dessert. An extra scoop for the President.

Benjamin: Will that be all, sir?

The President: Yes, and a terrific job tonight, Benjamin. I'm sure your father is looking down from Heaven right now, mighty proud.

Benjamin exits.

— End of Transcript —

Follow-up:

March 18.

Laura Ingraham touts hydroxychloroquine on her nightly news show.

March 19

During his coronavirus Task Force briefing, Trump mentions the drug for the first time.

March 21

Trump goes on Twitter and promotes the combination of hydroxychloroquine and Azithromycin, announcing, "One of the biggest game changers in the history of medicine."

March 23

Trump retweets a Fox News story on the effective use of the drug and brings it up again in the daily coronavirus briefing. "At my direction, the federal government is working to help obtain large quantities of chloroquine... the combination of hydroxychloroquine and the Z-Pak I think as a combination is looking very, very good." He also tells a story about a man who was about to die, was given the drug, and "woke up soon after in really good shape."

March 28

The FDA provides emergency authorization for hydroxychloroquine as a treatment for COVID-19.

March 29

At a briefing in the Rose Garden, Trump thanks the FDA for its quick approval of the drug.

March 30

Trump goes on *Fox & Friends* to say, "Hydroxychloroquine is a very powerful drug and we're going to know within days... which is going to be very exciting if something positive comes of it. But that's being tested very strongly in New York... We have over a thousand people on the drug together with Z-Pak..."

Later, Department of Health and Human Services Secretary Alex Azar announced the government has obtained 31 million tablets from two drug companies. Trump adds that another company has donated 6 million doses to hospitals across the country.

April 1

Dr. Fauci cautions that controlled studies are still needed to test the efficacy of the drug.

Sweden announces a study that shows "serious side effects" from the use of hydroxychloroquine.

April 3

At a briefing, Trump says: "Hydroxychloroquine — I don't know, but it's looking like it's having some good results... that would be a phenomenal thing... could have pretty big impacts and we'll see what happens."

That night, Laura Ingraham brings two doctors with her to the White House to meet with Trump to continue promoting the drug.

April 4

Trump again hypes the drug during daily briefings, announcing the national strategic stockpile now has 29 million doses of the medication. "We've having some very good things happening with it and we're going to be distributing it — we're going to be distributing it through the Strategic National Stockpile." He concludes: "Hydroxychloroquine — try it, if you'd like."

April 7

A reporter asks Trump about the drug's side effects, including heart failure. Trump's answer: "The side effects are the least of it. You have people dying all over the place... and generally the side effects having to do with the heart are really with the Z-Pak having to do with the heart, not with the hydroxychloroquine."

That night, he calls Sean Hannity on air to tell the news host that "countries with malaria problems, and who take the drug, don't seem to have a problem with the virus."

April 11

Brazil stops its study of chloroquine due to concerns of side effects. "Our study raises enough red flags to halt its use in order to avoid more unnecessary deaths."

April 13

Trump hawks hydroxychloroquine during his daily briefing: “Just recently, a friend of mine told me he got better because of the use of that — that drug. So, who knows? And you combine it with Z-Pak, you combine it with Zinc — depending on your doctor’s recommendation. And it’s having some very good results, I’ll tell you.”

“I think if anybody recommended it other than me,” he added, “it would be used all over the place, to be honest with you. I think the fact that I recommended it, I probably set it back a lot. But it’s a lot of good things that are happening with it. A lot of good tests.”

April 18

Trump retweets a conservative website that claims the President’s “gamble on hydroxychloroquine appears to be paying off.”

April 21

Damning results from a study conducted by the Department of Veteran Affairs suggest that those treated with hydroxychloroquine or hydroxychloroquine and Azithromycin didn't see marked improvement from use of the drugs. In fact, the rate of death was higher in groups treated with the drugs than among those who didn't receive the treatment.

April 22

Rick Bright, the former director of the Biomedical Advanced Research and Development Authority, alleges that he was demoted because he objected to the administration's promotion of chloroquine and hydroxychloroquine. "I rightly resisted efforts to provide an unproven drug on demand to the American public," he wrote in a statement.

"Well, I've never heard of him," Trump said of Bright at the daily briefing. "If the guy says he was pushed out of a job, maybe he was, maybe he wasn't. I — you'd have to hear the other side. I don't know who he is."

April 23

Trump is asked why he's stopped promoting hydroxychloroquine. "I haven't at all. I haven't at all... We had some results and they perhaps aren't so good... but I also read many good results as well."

April 24

The FDA formally warns against taking the medicines Trump has promoted due to "serious heart rhythm problems."

By April 25, Fox News, with Laura Ingraham leading the way, hydroxychloroquine and chloroquine as a cure and/or treatment for COVID-19 had been mentioned over 1,500 times.

On April 28, the United States reported over 1 million cases of coronavirus and more than 57,000 deaths.

* * *

CHAPTER 4

PHONE CALL TO SENATOR LINDSEY GRAHAM

It was Sunday, May 6 and the President sat nude at his makeup table checking the white circles around his eyes. He needed to find smaller goggles to wear during his tanning sessions, he thought to himself.

The landline rang and Trump picked up. "Senator Graham is holding," said the White House operator.

Lindsey Graham — Senior Senator from South Carolina — said brightly, "I thought you'd be on the links today, Mr. President. It's a beautiful day."

Trump cut right to the business at hand. "I wanted to ask you about what's going on with Burr." That was Senator Richard Burr of North Carolina, who had just stepped down as Chairman of the Intelligence Committee while the FBI investigated charges of insider trading.

"I'm sure you know more about what's going on than I do," said Graham.

"Terrible thing — using inside information to dump stocks just after you left an Intelligence briefing."

"Especially when Burr told the public the virus is nothing to worry about," agreed Graham.

"And can you believe that bimbo Loeffler from Georgia? Sells $15 million in stocks after the same briefing. Then says it was... what, a coincidence? I told Kemp she was bad news."

"Sure seems like she got some 'splainin' to do," joshed Graham.

"Any idea who Mitch is going to pick to replace Burr?"

Graham: "Well, I'm sure Mitch'll play it close to the vest per usual, but I think it's going to be Rubio."

Trump was disappointed. He was hoping it'd be Cornyn from Texas — someone Trump knew he could wind around his little finger when he had to. "Why Rubio?" he asked.

"I'm sure Mitch has his reasons."

"And what happens to Burr's report? The one he and Warner have been working on. That Russian-hoax thing."

"Oh, it'll just proceed normally. But I wouldn't worry about it, Mr. President. Judiciary's got your back." *(Author's note: Lindsey Graham was Chairman of the Judiciary Committee.)*

"And how's that going?" asked Trump.

"Trust me, Mr. President — come October, we'll have everything we need to blow Biden right out of the water."

"I hope so. Hunter Biden walks out of China with $1.5 billion and nobody gives a shit. And then Biden says he never talked about his son's overseas business dealings. You know that's a lie. Then Hunter's suddenly working for Burisma in the Ukraine at $50,000 a month and he knows nothing about energy while his father's making all those deals. They should both be in jail."

"Don't you worry, Mr. President," said Graham, "come October you'll have all the ammunition you need. Now get out there and whack those golf balls."

Trump hung up, thinking for a minute that he'd call Rubio, but decided against it. He never liked Rubio. Not since that debate when Rubio had made fun of his hands. And what was it he said after that? Small hands mean a small "you know what."

Trump got up and checked himself — full frontal — in the mirror. No problem there, he said to himself. Could have been a porn star if he wanted. It was perfect. Like that phone call. Why, he'd stand his penis up against any man in America. More than a few women had trembled at the very sight of it. And one of his former wives — he couldn't remember which — had even called him The Elephant Man.

* * *

CHAPTER 5

PHONE CALL TO DONALD JR.

May 16, 2020.

It was a little past 6:00 a.m. when Donald Trump Jr. reached out, half asleep, to pick up his chiming cell phone. He did not have to check the ID to know it was his father calling. And why.

Last night, Don Jr. had posted an Instagram to his 2.6 million followers implying that Joe Biden was a pedophile, along with videos of Biden touching young children (carefully edited from their parents' public swearing-in ceremonies). Don Jr. had written, "See you later, alligator. After a while, pedophile."

"Hi, Pop," said Don Jr. after clearing his throat so he'd sound like he'd been up and hard at work for hours.

"That Instagram you sent. Your sister told me she thought it crossed the line," Trump said gruffly.

"It was a joke. Can't anyone take a joke? Didn't she see the smiling emoji?"

"Well, stay on message. Biden's old and out of it and feeble. Remember?"

"Okay, Pop. But you got to admit it was funny."

But the President — on to more important phone calls — had hung up.

Don Jr. lay his head back on his MyPillow, one of the hundreds Mike Lindell, MyPillow inventor and Trump donor, had sent to the Trump family for Christmas.

Don Jr.'s girlfriend, Kimberly Guilfoyle, stirred beside him. "Was your father upset about the Instagram?" she asked throatily.

"Naw, Pooh Bear (his pet name for her), he's just sorry he didn't think of it himself," said Don Jr., reaching to pull her closer. "Guess who just woke up?" he said with a mischievous grin.

“The Trumpster?” she giggled.

“The one and only,” he said, guiding her hand down his hairless chest.

* * *

CHAPTER 6

POMPEO COMES TO DINNER

On May 19, leaks to the press revealed that Secretary of State Mike Pompeo (with wife Susan) had been holding "intimate dinners" at taxpayers' expense in the historic reception rooms at the State Department.

There had been a total of twenty-four dinners that had begun shortly after Pompeo was sworn in as Secretary of State from July 2018 to February 2020.

These events were called "Madison Dinners," named after the fourth President James Madison, known for inviting foreign diplomats to exchange ideas over gala and elaborate meals.

Pompeo's guest list was a hefty collection of the global elite: Congresspeople, Senators, megadonors, members of the Saudi Royal Family, and celebrities from the media. Some of the more prominent names included Supreme

Court Justices Alito and Gorsuch, Bush strategist Karl Rove, Fox News personalities Laura Ingraham and Brian Kilmeade, race car driver Dale Earnhardt Jr., hedge-fund executive Paul Singer, Chick-fil-A CEO Bubba Cathy, Home Depot founder Ken Langone, Texas real estate tycoon Harlon Crow, Raytheon CEO Thomas Kennedy, Republican power couple Matt and Mercedes Schlapp (whose money funded the campaign against same-sex marriage), Marjorie Dannenfelser, president of the Susan B. Anthony List, an anti-abortion organization... and two Saudi diplomats, Fahid al-Thumairy and Musaed Ahmed al-Jarrah, named by the FBI as funding at least three of the 9/11 hijackers.

A “Madison Dinner” typically began around 6:00 p.m. when guests arrived at the driveway of the Harry S. Truman Building, the headquarters of U.S. diplomacy, where State Department officials escorted them to a special elevator reserved for the evening.

Upstairs on the 8th floor, guests were given a tour of the historic Diplomatic Reception

Rooms that include the Benjamin Franklin State Dining Room, the Martha Washington Ladies Lounge, and the John Quincy Adams State Drawing Room.

After cocktails (accompanied by a harpist), the guests were seated for dinner, which lasted a little over an hour and began with toasts from Pompeo and his wife.

The menu reflected that night's theme. For example, in February — in honor of Mardi Gras — the guests were served Chicken Andouille Gumbo, Crawfish Etouffee, mini-crab cakes with Cajun sauce, and King cake, a New Orleans tradition, with a baby figurine baked inside.

To celebrate George Washington's birthday, the Pompeos had their chef duplicate the menu once served by the first President at one of his famous Thursday dinners at Mount Vernon: poached salmon, roast beef, wild duck, lettuce and cucumber salad, peas, artichokes, and mince pies, assorted tarts, puddings, and custard.

Pompeo sent his guests into gales of laughter when he told them that because George had such bad teeth, all the food served at Mount Vernon was soft and easy to chew.

Guests were seated at one round table in front of the fireplace. Under its mantel were these words:

I Pray Heaven *To Bestow*
THE BEST OF BLESSING ON
This House
And All *that shall hereafter* Inhabit *it.*
May None but Honest *and* Wise Men *ever rule under* This Roof.

Those words had been written in 1800 by John Adams when he arrived in the new federal city of Washington, D.C. In the final year of World War II, Franklin Roosevelt had them inscribed in gold just under the fireplace mantel in the State Dining Room.

But Pompeo's dinners stopped immediately after Trump got wind of them. It wasn't that the President was upset that Pompeo was spending taxpayer money in an obvious effort to shore up support for his eventual run for President in 2024. No — it was simply that Pompeo's invitation had been drawn from the President's own database of rich donors — donors Trump considered his and his alone.

Trump never confronted Pompeo directly about the dinners. Instead, he had his Chief of Staff Mark Meadows make a short, one-minute phone call: "The Boss says knock off the fuckin' dinners."

Trump, of course, was pissed that someone in his administration was running for President besides himself, even if it was for 2024.

Later, at a quiet lunch at the White House with Jared and Ivanka, Trump was still annoyed: "I can't believe that Pompeo finished first in his class at West Point," he told them. "That had to be the worst class in history." Then he added: "I should have gone to West Point. I would have graduated a General."

* * *

CHAPTER 7

TRUMP'S OUTREACH TO AFRICAN AMERICANS

In 2016, Trump managed to get 8% of the black vote — just enough to help carry him to victory in key swing states. But by early April 2020, poll numbers showed Trump's approval ratings among African Americans slipping at an alarming rate.

To counter this trend, Senior Campaign Advisers suggested a major address to the nation laying out his position on race and race relations in America, while reminding the black community all he had done for them so far.

Instead, Trump came up with a more informal approach: a round-table discussion before a friendly black audience at the Universal-Global Baptist Church outside Mobile, Alabama.

The following are recorded excerpts of that meeting, with leaders from the African-American community, on May 26, 2020:

PRESIDENT TRUMP

(after applause)

Well, I want to thank you very much. We're here today with some of the black leaders of our country and — people that are highly respected for the most part, and have been working with me right from the beginning. And we've done a lot. Believe me. We've done criminal justice reform. We got a lot of great black people out of jail.

(applause)

We had the best unemployment numbers for blacks until the virus from China. We did things people didn't think possible. So what I think

I do is — for the media in the back — go down the dais and everyone can do a quick introduction of each other and then say something about all the great things I've done. I'll start with me. I'm Donald Trump and I'm President of the United States.

(audience laughter, applause)

AUDIENCE

Four more years! Four more years! Four more years!

PRESIDENT TRUMP

And now our host, Pasture of this beautiful mega church, Pasture Mantan Money.

MANTAN MONEY

Thank you, Mr. President. It's an honor to have you here at our

8,500-seat sanctuary. Now you may not know this, but only fifteen years ago I was conducting services in my kitchen and then I read *The Art of the Deal* by Donald J. Trump and today I preach to a congregation of over 30,000 with over $80 million in revenue per year. I also have two Bentleys, a private jet, and three homes — one in Mobile, one in New Jersey, and one in New York — worth more than $3 million apiece. So thank you, Mr. President.

PRESIDENT TRUMP

Well, I know this. A well-educated black has a tremendous advantage over a well-educated white in terms of today's job market. If I were starting off today, I'd love being a well-educated black because they do have an actual advantage. Terrence? Please?

TERRENCE K. WILLIAMS

I am comedian Terrence K. Williams
and I am sitting next to the greatest
President since Abraham Lincoln.

PRESIDENT TRUMP

Well, you know there's a lot of people
who aren't too sure about Lincoln.
I mean, there's two sides — right?
Some say he didn't do that much
really, but I'm going to take a pass on
honest Abe — as they called him —
but I have to say, I've done more than
any President since. Angela?

ANGELA STANTON-KING

My name is Angela Stanton-King.
I am founder of the American King
Foundation, a member of the Board
of Directors for 'Black Voices for
Trump'. I'm currently running for
Congressperson in Georgia to replace

Democratic representative John Lewis and I was recently pardoned by the greatest President ever!

(audience applause)

PRESIDENT TRUMP

Unless it's General Flynn, nobody deserved a pardon more than you. When I heard you got two years for running a stolen car ring, I couldn't believe it. And with my support, you are going to unseat John Lewis, who represents one of the worst-run and most-dangerous districts anywhere in the United States, right after the district of Elijah Cummings in South Carolina.

(audience applause)

You know, most Congressmen are in office first, then they go to jail. I'm pleased to see that you've decided to do it the other way 'round.

(scattered audience applause)

JACK BREWER

My name is Jack Brewer. I am a former free safety for the Vikings, Giants, and Eagles. And President of the NFL Players for Trump. And I can only say, Mr. President, that in my humble opinion, you are this country's first black President.

(audience applause)

PRESIDENT TRUMP

And let me tell you, when Jack was playing, he didn't take a knee when they played the National Anthem. No sir. He stood proud with his head down and one hand on his heart. Not like those 'sons of bitches' today who want to demean our flag and great heritage. I just wish I was one of their owners so I could say 'You're fired.'

PASTOR SCOTT

I'm Pastor Darrell Scott of the New Spirit Revival Center in Cleveland, Ohio and a founding member of the National Diversity Coalition for Trump. And I believe what this guy here is doing. I'm onboard the Trump train all the way! And I want you to know that I have talked to street gangs — the Crips and the Bloods — in Cleveland, Chicago, and St. Louis — and they have agreed to lower the 'body count' because of the good work you've done in their neighborhoods.

PRESIDENT TRUMP

Thank you, Reverend. That's always nice to hear. And you have to hand it to Reverend Scott. It was his idea to hand out large sums of cash — I heard up to tens of thousands of dollars — at local Trump rallies to lucky black attendees. Great idea.

ALVEDA KING

I'm evangelist Alveda King and niece of Martin Luther King Jr. and executive director of Civil Rights for the Unborn. And I want to thank you, Mr. President, for bringing back the coal mines, freeing convicted felons, and saving all those little babies in the womb.

(audience applause)

PRESIDENT TRUMP

Thank you, Alveda. And I know that your uncle Martin Luther King is looking down on us right now, saying what a great job we are all doing for black people in this country.

KATRINA PIERSON

I'm Katrina Pierson, Senior Adviser to the President's Reelection Campaign, here in support of all the great work the President is doing, and I've been with Donald Trump from the very beginning because I knew that if we elected him President, we could deliver a generation of black children a real shot at the American dream. And every day that I go to my office at Trump Campaign headquarters, I know I'm doing God's work.

DR. BEN CARSON

I'm Dr. Ben Carson. Secretary of Housing and Human Services. And I want to thank the President for giving me the opportunity to serve my country under a great leader like Donald Trump. A man who doesn't see color.

ALVEDA KING

That's right. He only sees red, white, and blue!

MANTAN MONEY

And green!

(audience applause and laughter)

PRESIDENT TRUMP

Thank you, everybody. And just let me say — I have always had good relationships with blacks. Or African Americans. I call them both. It doesn't matter to me. I remember when they used to be called 'colored people'. That's where the NAACP comes from. National Association for the Advancement of Colored People. A lot of people don't know that. When I was only a boy, 11, maybe 12, I used to go with my father Fred Trump when he collected rent from many colored people. The first of every month, he'd be there — rain or shine — with a big smile on his face and an open hand. My father, as big as he was professionally, never sent anyone else to collect the rent. He went himself. He went himself because he cared about the people who lived in his hundreds of buildings and what they were up to. And he didn't see color. It didn't matter if you were brown, black, or yellow as long as you paid your rent. And that little boy who tagged along — that little boy grew up to be me. Your President of the United States.

AUDIENCE

(chants)

Four more years! Four more years! Four more years!

PRESIDENT TRUMP

When I was doing *Celebrity Apprentice*, I always made sure there were black people on the show. I even wanted to have one contest between all-black celebrities and all-white celebrities, but NBC said no. Which was too bad because that show would have had the highest ratings ever. And we got some pretty high ratings. Twelve million viewers in my final season. And we always had black celebrities. Lil Jon, Vivica

A. Fox, Arsenio Hall, and Dennis Rodman. And let me tell you this — it was Dennis Rodman who first got me interested in North Korea. Way before I was President, he told me that this guy — Kim Jong-un — wasn't as bad as the liberal press made him out to be. Of course, Dennis had no idea I'd be President one day, he just wanted me to go there to check out some beach-front property. A lot of people don't know this, but North Korea has some of the most beautiful undeveloped beach property in the world. I told Kim — right after I took a tour — I said, you know, if you put up a couple of luxury hotels with a couple of golf courses, this could be another Miami Beach. I told Kim — I'm the only person in the world who calls him by his first name — I can't believe you haven't built here. By the way, most people don't know what a great sense of humor Kim has. I'm telling you, when he tells the story about how he killed his uncle you almost fall out of your chair laughing so hard. Of course, if I hadn't been President, we'd be in a nuclear war right now with North Korea, so Dennis Rodman gets a lot of credit. Because if Obama had been President another year, that's what you'd have with North Korea — a nuclear war — which I prevented. Because when I told Kim all about the new kind of nuclear weapons we had perfected, his hair stood on end... and that's some hair to stand on end, believe me. But if it had been Obama, there'd be a war. And it's because of Obama — totally weak — there won't be another black president for generations. First day I stepped into the Oval Office, my Generals came to me and said 'Sir, we're out of ammunition.' They like to say 'sir'. That's how Obama left our great Army, Navy, Marines, Air Force, and Coast Guard. <u>Now</u> when I see them,

I say have you enough ammunition and they say 'Yes, sir. Thanks to you, sir.' But the media won't report that. The media standing back there won't tell you the great work I'm doing. The media won't tell you — and this is something I don't talk about — but I give my salary — it's $450,000 a year. I give it back and surprisingly they don't think any other President in history has ever given their salary. It's $450,000.

(the audience "wows")

PRESIDENT TRUMP

It comes quarterly and I guarantee if I was ever late in giving it back — it would be a front-page story. But the press isn't going to write that. I'm losing billions on this job, but you don't hear about that either. You know what my legal fees are a year? I'll tell you: tens of millions of dollars a year defending myself against scum. And then they say I get rich on this. They say an Arab goes into one of my hotels and spends $500 a night for a room and they say 'Trump's getting rich.' I'm losing billions a year and the Fake Media says I'm getting rich on Arabs renting rooms. These are very dishonest people. But we do things. And you people have made such progress — making tremendous progress. So I want to thank all of you black people for coming here today. I appreciate everyone in this room. When I think of all you've gone through and now you're making a comeback like nobody's ever seen before. You had the worst crime. You had the worst neighborhoods. You had the worst jobs. You had the lowest housing ownerships... And now, as your President, you've come a long way. A long ways at winning, winning, winning. But I don't get credit for it. The press doesn't write about it. But we appreciate you being here. We appreciate everybody in this room. Thank you.

(audience gives him a standing ovation; Trump motions them to sit)

PRESIDENT TRUMP

Now before we leave here today, I'd like to recognize some of my very good black friends who are with us in the audience. First, my good friend Kanye West. Kanye, stand up and take a bow. Kanye has just been named to the Forbes 100 of the richest black entrepreneurs in the country. He's making so much money, Oprah is tearing out her wig. Take a bow, Kanye.

(audience applause)

PRESIDENT TRUMP

I'd also like to thank my good black friend, radio show host Larry Elder, for being here today. A man who's been black all his life.

(audience applause)

A lot of people don't even know that Larry is Negro — that's how well he talks. Also in the audience is the terrific comedian and wrestler — a very funny man — from the Greg Gutfeld Show, stand up, Tyrus.

(audience applause)

Big, big man. How'd you like to see him throw a heckler out of one of my rallies, huh? And last, another of my great black friends with us today, Frederick Douglass... Frederick, stand up and take a bow. What? Oh, sorry. I just found out that Fred — great name Fred, my father's name was Fred — couldn't be here today because of other business. Sorry, I wasn't told about that... Anyway, that about does it. Thank you all for coming. Thank you very much.

(a second standing ovation from the audience)

Back on Air Force One — on his way to the White House — Trump stepped out of the washroom still drying his hands and, catching the eye of Mark Meadows, said, "Can you believe those people? They really think Jesus Christ is coming back one day. Well, I have a bridge in Brooklyn I'd like to sell them."

* * *

CHAPTER 8

GEORGE FLOYD'S DEATH, THE PROTESTS, AND TRUMP'S RESPONSE

On Memorial Day, May 25, an unarmed black man named George Floyd was killed — while handcuffed — by a Minneapolis police officer. Videos of the tragedy were on the news three days later. When asked if he had seen the video — which showed one of the arresting officers with his knee pressed to Mr. Floyd's neck for over eight minutes — Trump replied: "I've seen it. Bad. Very bad. I watched it with Melania. She couldn't look. But then, there could be other angles. You know, a different camera might show something else. You never know."

When Hope Hicks told the President that Joe Biden would be attending George Floyd's funeral, Trump asked if he would be speaking. "Not that I know of," she replied.

"Too bad," Trump said. "You know he's going to say something dumb."

"The only person speaking I know of is the Reverend Al Sharpton."

Trump: "I've known Sharpton for years. From New York. Ran into him a lot. Not a bad guy. But I liked him more when he was fat. I like my black ministers fat."

That night, Senator Lindsey Graham called on Trump's private phone. "I have a joke for you, Mr. President," Graham began. "I figured you could use a laugh about now."

"I'll bite."

"How did they know that the $20 bill George Floyd was trying to pass was a counterfeit?"

"How?" asked Trump, who as a rule did not like jokes very much.

"It had a picture of Harriet Tubman on it."

Trump faked a small laugh, then quickly changed the subject to Graham's investigation into the Bidens.

By May 31, cities across the nation erupted in protests — led by Black Lives Matter — over the death of George Floyd. How to react prompted a clear division among Trump's Senior Advisers:

There were those, like Don Jr., who advocated a powerful "law-and-order" message and those (like Kushner) who were concerned about alienating undecided black voters.

It was, in fact, Kushner who had cautioned Trump about his recent rhetoric regarding the protesters outside the White House.

For example, Trump's statement that "If they had breached the fence, they would have been greeted with the most vicious dogs and most ominous weapons I have ever seen. That's when people would have been really badly hurt, at best."

When Jared told Ivanka that he was troubled by his father-in-law's message that the Secret Service had vicious dogs to "sic" on the protesters, Ivanka replied, "Oh, that's just the Adderall talking."

Nobody on Team Trump had to be reminded that in 2016 Hillary Clinton's failure to get the black turnout in the same numbers Obama got was a decisive mistake, propelling Trump to small victories in swing states like Michigan and Pennsylvania.

Rather than go after the black "looters," Kushner suggested they link Biden to the 1994 Crime Bill which resulted in the incarceration of a decade of young black men. The same attack they had leveled successfully against Hillary.

But as the peaceful protests turned ugly with widespread rioting and looting, it wasn't difficult to predict that it was only a matter of time before Trump unleashed the full fury of his right-wing playbook.

The turning point came on Friday night, May 29. As crowds of protesters grew outside the White House, the Secret Service — out of an abundance of caution — moved Trump, his wife, and son to a secure bunker below ground.

When word leaked to the press that Donald Trump had been rushed by the Secret Service to the bunker, the shit hit the fan.

The image of Trump hunkered down in fear of the demonstrators outside the White House, chanting their outrage over George Floyd's murder, warped the President's campaign narrative as the tough, all-powerful strongman.

It was supposed to be Biden who was locked down in his basement, afraid to be seen — not Trump.

Trump and his Senior Advisers determined they needed an immediate response by the next news cycle.

Sunday, calls went out to Secretary of Defense Mark Esper, Attorney General Barr, and the Chairman of the Joint Chiefs of Staff, General Mark Milley.

Acting on orders from Trump, Chief of Staff Meadows ordered all three men to report to the Oval Office Monday morning, 9:00 a.m. sharp, prepared to spend the day. An evolving battle plan was now taking shape.

Stephen Miller was tasked to write a five-to-ten-minute speech outlining Trump's response to George Floyd's death and the rioting and looting that had taken place around the country the past few days.

Meanwhile, VP Pence was told to set up a conference call with the governors of all fifty states.

On Monday morning, June 1, surrounded by Pence, Esper, Kushner, Hope Hicks, AG Barr, Chief of Staff Meadows, and four-star General Milley, Trump got on the phone with the governors. He got off to a somewhat rambling start: "People are here that you'll be seeing a lot of. General Milley is here. He's head of the Joint Chiefs of Staff, a fighter, a war hero, a lot of victories and no losses and he hates to see the way it's being handled in the various states and I just put him in charge. The Attorney General is here, Bill Barr, and we will activate Bill Barr and activate him very strongly. The Secretary of Defense is here. We're strongly looking for arrests. You have to get much tougher... you have to dominate. If you don't dominate, you're wasting your time. They're going to run all over you, you'll look like a bunch of jerks. You have to dominate, and you have to arrest people, and you have to try people and they have to go to jail for long periods of time."

The theme of Trump's message was clear: dominate the protesters, dominate the streets — and those governors who didn't were "fools and jerks."

Only five of the governors responded and only one really pushed back and that was Pritzker of Illinois. *(Author's note: Many governors, including Cuomo of New York, Newsom of California, and Murphy of New Jersey, had already jumped off the line.)* Here's Pritzker's testy exchange with the President:

GOVERNOR PRITZKER

Can you hear me okay? (INAUDIBLE)

PRESIDENT TRUMP

Go ahead.

GOVERNOR PRITZKER

Thank you, Mr. President. I wanted to take this moment, I can't let it pass to (INAUDIBLE) to say that I'm extraordinarily concerned with the rhetoric that's been used by you, it's been inflammatory and not okay... We have to call for calm... and the rhetoric that's coming out of the White House is making it worse.

PRESIDENT TRUMP

Well, thank you very much, Jay. I don't like your rhetoric either...

When a female voice announced that there was no one else in the queue, the President concluded the call this way:

PRESIDENT TRUMP

Okay, I want to thank all of you, be strong, be tough, be smart... Many, many people, you know, worry about Mr. Floyd, but there are many other people who have been badly hurt and killed and the way we're going to do it, the way we're going to stop the problem is to be strong, you have to be strong. Use our National Guard, you're much better off with too many than too few. Too few is unacceptable, so go out there and get 'em, good luck tonight, and thank you very much.

During the conference call, Trump interrupted at different times to ask his Chief of Staff Mark Meadows — former Congressman from North Carolina — to fetch him things such as a Diet Pepsi, a new Sharpie, and a Twix bar. All to the embarrassment of Barr, Esper, and General Milley, who couldn't remember seeing a grown white man ordered around that way.

After a take-out lunch of Big Macs and fries served in the Oval Office, Trump and his team revised the first draft of Miller's speech. VP Pence and Secretary of Defense Esper argued that it should invoke the Insurrection Act of 1807 that would allow the President to send U.S. military to quell the nationwide protests.

Arguing against it were AG Barr and General Milley, both concerned with states' rights and assuring the President that there was sufficient force in the capital to secure the city.

Barr had, by then, activated a host of law-enforcement agencies ready to spring into action at his say-so: the Park Police, Secret Service assault teams, the National Guard, ICE, agents from Homeland Security, guards from federal prisons in Texas and Utah, FBI Hostage Rescue Teams, and a small squad of Black Hawk helicopters.

All that was missing, joked Barr, were the Navy SEALs that had taken down Osama bin Laden.

After Trump agreed that he would delay announcing the implementation of the Insurrection Act, the press was alerted that the President would address the nation in the Rose Garden at 6:15.

It was then that Trump came up with the idea that after his speech he would visit the Episcopal Church of St. John. A block from the White House, the church had suffered minor fire damage to its basement the previous Friday. Built in 1816, it is known as the Presidents' church.

"We need a big finish" was the way Trump put it. "Maybe I could even hold up a Bible. A big Bible."

The idea was warmly seconded by Ivanka, Jared, and Hope Hicks, who immediately scurried off in search of the appropriate prop — a perfect visual reminder of Trump's devotion to the word of God.

There was only one problem: the space in front of the church was presently occupied by a couple hundred demonstrators.

AG Barr — now tieless, having spilled McDonald's special sauce on himself during lunch — went out with his aides to inspect the area in front of the church. It soon became obvious to Barr that Lafayette Park had to be cleared of demonstrators before Trump could make his visit to St. John's.

Back in the White House, Barr gave the go-ahead to his rapidly swelling mélange of troops.

At exactly 6:17, Barr's army advanced on the protesters, firing flash-bang grenades, rubber bullets, and canisters of tear gas. Overhead, a low-flying Black Hawk helicopter swooped above the fleeing crowd, making the kind of maneuvers usually reserved for scaring Honduran refugees.

Meanwhile, a block away, at 6:43 Trump began his speech in the Rose Garden. After spending a few sentences on the "brutal death of George Floyd," Trump got to the red meat of his statement:

PRESIDENT TRUMP

> I am your president of law and order and an ally of all peaceful protesters. But in recent days, our nation has been gripped by professional anarchists, violent mobs, arsonists, looters, criminals, rioters. Antifa and others... These are not actors of peaceful protest, these are acts of domestic terror... If mayors and governors refuse to establish an overwhelming law-enforcement presence... then I will deploy the United States military — and quickly — to solve the problem for them... I am also taking swift and decisive action to protect our great capital, Washington, D.C. I am dispatching thousands and thousands of heavily armed soldiers, military personnel, and law-enforcement officers

> to stop the looting, vandalism, and wanton destruction of property... I take these actions today with firm resolve and with a true and passionate love for our country. By far our greatest days lie ahead. Thank you very much, and now I'm going to pay my respects to a very, very special place.

With that, Trump turned abruptly and reentered the White House, only to emerge on the North Side and walk out through the gates to St. John's (where he hadn't been since his Inauguration Day). Following the President was a small phalanx of Cabinet officers, White House staff, and Senior Advisers — Barr, Esper, Meadows, Jared, Ivanka (conspicuously carrying a Prada tote bag, retail $4,500), and the Joint Chief of Staff in battle fatigues, looking like he'd just gotten off a plane from Fallujah.

Trailing behind them was the new Press Secretary Kayleigh McEnany, who wore a silver cross around her neck, which some say she used to hold in front of her whenever she saw Jared Kushner stepping out of his open coffin.

After Barr pointed out the boarded-up church, Trump stopped in front of it. Ivanka reached into her bag, took out a very large Bible, and handed it to him. Trump held the Bible up for the cameras — backwards as if it were read from right to left — like it was in Hebrew.

When a reporter asked if it was his Bible, Trump ad-libbed: "It's a Bible."

The Bible itself had come from Jay Sekulow who used it to find loopholes in the Sermon on the Mount.

After urging from the President, Barr, Meadows, Esper, and McEnany joined the President in front of the church for more photos. Then all headed home to the White House.

Trump led the pack, musing to himself that it had all gone perfectly. He was especially pleased for having come up with the idea of the Bible and couldn't wait to get to the Oval Office and the phone calls that would be coming in from ministers across the country congratulating him for his Christian reverence.

Lost in thought, Trump never noticed, as he walked by, the graffiti on the wall of the church: Fuck Trump.

* * *

CHAPTER 9

PHONE CALL FROM THE PRESIDENT TO THE AG

It was the night of June 15 and Attorney General William Barr was sound asleep in his McLean, Virginia mansion (one he designed himself) when his BlackBerry rang. Immediately, he knew it was the President and why he was calling. As Barr reached for the phone, his wife of forty-seven years, Christine, woke, sat up, and turned on the night-stand light on her side of the bed.

Laying there — in his striped pajamas — backlit by the moon — Barr looked rounder than usual. His face fleshier and pudgy. Even his jowls had jowls. It was the kind of face you might see behind the counter of a Catholic bookstore around the corner from St. Patrick's.

"Yes, Mr. President?" said Barr.

"What in hell's going on with this fucking book?" The use of the word "fucking," Barr had learned, was a sure sign the President was upset. The book, of course, was John Bolton's *The Room Where It Happened.* Bolton had been Trump's National Security Adviser for seventeen months before he either quit or was fired (depending on who you believed). Prior to that, Bolton had been an occasional pundit on Fox News, best known for a mustache you'd expect to see on an actor playing Ekdal in *The Wild Duck.*

In his book, Bolton claimed, among other things, that Trump had begged China's President Xi Jinping to help him win the 2020 election by buying soybeans and pork to help carry Midwestern farm states.

"We've already sought the injunction, Mr. President," replied Barr calmly.

"I had Sekulow call the publisher. Karp I think his name is from Simon & Schuster. You know, one Jew to another."

"I believe Jay Sekulow is a born-again Christian."

"Once a Jew, always a Jew," snorted Trump. "Anyway, Sekulow said the book's already in print. And there's nothing we can do."

"I agree. I'm afraid an injunction may indeed be moot."

"Mute? What do you mean mute?"

"I said moot. That is, a lawsuit against the publisher may be too late, given the book's already been shipped. News outlets already have copies."

Out of habit, Christine reached for her rosary on the night stand and began nervously fingering the beads.

Trump continued full blast: "That fuckin' washed-up Bolton. I gave him a job when no one else would and look what he does to me. I want him arrested. Charged. For revealing classified information. Don't we have a case there?"

"Well, there is the Espionage Act. You could have Mike Ellis go through the book and give me the violations. That'd help."

"You'll get that today. I want him charged. Locked up. That wacko, disgruntled sick puppy. All he wanted to do was go to war. Iran. China. Venezuela. North Korea. He didn't give a shit. As long as he got a fuckin' war," Trump blustered. "'Walrus face' I used to call him."

"You make some very good points, Mr. President. You would have made a great lawyer."

"The man's a fuckin' liar," continued Trump. "I never said I thought Finland was part of Russia. What I said was Russia didn't need to invade Finland because they already had places just as cold."

"I'll do what the law allows, Mr. President."

Both men hung up simultaneously.

Trump's voice was loud enough that Christine had heard everything. "I thought John Bolton was your friend?" she asked.

"He is," said the AG.

"And you're actually going to put him in jail?"

"Not much chance of that. Though I might be able to freeze his royalties for a while."

"Such language. For a President."

"He's upset because Bolton wrote that Trump said Finland was part of Russia."

"What a nitwit."

"I know. But he's our nitwit," said Barr in that understated way of his.

Barr got out of bed and put on his robe and slippers.

"Where you going?" asked his wife.

"To the study," he said, "to relax."

"I truly hope you know what you're doing with that man," she called after him.

"I always know what I'm doing," said the Attorney General.

Within minutes, Christine Barr could hear the strains of bagpipes coming from downstairs. Her husband was playing his favorite tune "The Irish March."

On the floor beside the bed, Molly, their yellow Lab, howled in accompaniment.

"Now look what you've started," Mrs. Barr yelled down to her husband over the din.

Not that she was cross with him. Mrs. Barr was as devoted to the Attorney General as the Attorney General was devoted to Trump.

* * *

CHAPTER 10

THE FOCUS GROUP

It was not a coincidence that the Trump Campaign — using a shell organization called The Freedom and Unity Committee (FUC) — leased a floor at 1 Pierrepont Plaza in trendy Brooklyn Heights, site of Hillary Clinton's 2016 headquarters. It was their idea of an inside joke.

The Committee, headed by Lev Beckerman — former Colonel in Israel's secret service, the Mossad — was there to create, develop, and disseminate anti-Biden "news" stories that would eventually reach their audience through social media, right-wing talk-show hosts, and conspiracy-minded publications and websites.

On June 30, 2020, the Committee had arranged for a focus group of ten black men and women — ranging in age from 25 to 70 — all registered Democrats and likely to vote for Biden.

The strategy was to come up with anti-Biden theories that would appeal to black voters in the hopes of peeling off a sufficient number to affect the outcome in swing states like Michigan, Pennsylvania, Ohio, and Wisconsin.

It was the same strategy that had proved successful against Hillary in 2016. It was lower turnout among black voters that propelled Trump to eke out small victories in Pennsylvania and Michigan that otherwise would have been out of reach.

A black Moderator — pretending to be a Biden campaign employee — conducted the focus group. His job was to introduce five damaging news stories (not yet circulated) about Biden and ask the participants a series of questions about them. That is: 1) Did they think they were fake news? 2) Real news? or 3) They weren't sure one way or the other.

Everyone sat around a conference table: five on each side, with the Moderator at the head. Video cameras capturing every minute of the ninety-minute session were conspicuously placed about the room. At the far end was a projection screen for slides and short videos.

In an adjacent room, unknown to the participants, were Lev and his team watching it all through a two-way mirror.

After a fun, nonthreatening, open-ended, off-topic question that enabled everyone to develop a safe level of comfort, the Moderator introduced the following "news" items:

1) Biden's claim that he was born in Scranton, PA at St. Mary's Hospital on November 20, 1942 is false. The birth certificate was a forgery. In truth, he was born five years earlier in 1937, making him 83 years old — the oldest person to ever run for the presidency. The proof is that there is no record of a Joseph Biden being born in 1942, according to the *Scranton Times-Tribune.*

Five participants thought this was fake news. Three thought it was credible. Two had no opinion.

2) Joe Biden has been accused by some reputable news organizations as having a tendency to fondle preadolescent girls, some as

young as 10. To support that claim, participants were shown videos taken at ceremonies in which the Vice President "touched" the daughters of men and women he had just sworn into office.

In addition to the videos, the focus group was also told that a former White House staffer had privately made the accusation that Michelle Obama once gave orders that Biden was never to be left alone with her daughters Malia and Sasha.

Five participants thought that claim was fake. Two thought it credible. Three had no opinion.

3) Recently, a 51-year-old black woman named Josephine Williams came forward to say that she was Joe Biden's illegitimate daughter. Her story was that her mother Beulah Williams was working as a nighttime cleaning woman at City Hall in Wilmington, Delaware when Joe Biden was a member of the City Council and that they would often meet at night and have sexual intercourse in one of the janitorial closets. When asked why she hadn't come

forward earlier, Josephine replied that she didn't know about it until her mother told her the night she died. So Josephine had no idea who her father was until her mother's deathbed confession. Because Beulah loved Joe, she decided to never say anything because she knew the truth would ruin Biden's career.

Here, the Moderator showed a slide of Josephine when she was 27 next to a picture of Joe Biden when, in 1972, he was first elected to the Senate at age 29. The resemblance was striking. The black Josephine's nose, lips, and ears were almost identical to Joe's.

Two thought this was fake news. Six thought it was believable. Two had no opinion.

4) Because of Biden's continuing gaffes, misstatements, and memory lapses, Biden's wife Jill had a team of doctors (comprised of neurologists, psychologists, and psychiatrists) who, after their examination, determined that Biden was suffering from onset dementia. It was further stated he would be fully incapacitated by August, the time of the Democratic Convention. It was then suggested

that at the Convention, Biden's name would be withdrawn as the party's nominee and Dr. Jill Biden would announce that former President Obama would take his place, asking the delegates for a unanimous voice vote in favor of the substitution.

Four thought it fake news. Five thought it credible. One had no opinion.

5) In December 2013, Joe Biden and his son Hunter travelled to China aboard Air Force Two when Biden was Vice President. During the week-long trip in which the VP met with his Chinese counterparts about a controversial Chinese air-defense zone, Hunter went off on his own trying to raise money for a newly formed equity fund. It was during that period of time that Hunter Biden could not be located for at least seventy-two hours. Recent allegations have come to light (through leaked CIA classified documents) that Hunter Biden had in fact been arrested after having been found in bed with a dead prostitute who had overdosed on cocaine. It took a phone call from President Obama in Washington to President Xi Jinping

to hush up the incident and get Hunter released from jail. The present danger was that, should Biden be elected President, he would be subject to blackmail by the Chinese government.

Three thought this was fake news. Six thought it was credible. And one had no opinion.

In the next two weeks, Lev and his team would conduct similar focus groups with various demographics: Latinos, suburban women, and white high school dropouts. Once the team discovered which of the Biden "news stories" would prove most persuasive, the stories — slightly refined — would be distributed to an assortment of right-wing media outlets, including Breitbart News, Newsmax, QAnon, and the Drudge Report — along with sympathetic pundits like Glenn Beck, Alex Jones, Sebastian Gorka, and their Russian trolls.

* * *

CHAPTER 11

ANOTHER PHONE CALL FROM THE PRESIDENT TO THE AG

It was July 2 and Christine Barr was propped up in bed listening to "Bible Bedtime Stories" on her cell phone when her husband the Attorney General came in, a sour expression etched across his features.

"What's <u>he</u> calling about this time?" his wife asked, taking off her headset.

"He wants me to enjoin the distribution of his niece's book," said Bill Barr wearily, getting into his pajamas.

"My Lord," Barr's wife said, "if you went around trying to enjoin every book Trump didn't like, there wouldn't be time in the day to brush your teeth."

"Apparently, his niece wrote some very nasty things about him."

"That's the niece he had cut out of his father's will?"

"Yes. Mary Trump."

"Well, what did he expect — a Valentine's Day card?"

"She claimed that Trump paid a Jewish man named Joe Shapiro to take his SATs for him," said Barr, knotting the drawstring on his pajama bottoms.

Christine Barr let out a derisive whoop. "That's it?" she said in mock disbelief. "That's what he's upset about?" She continued: "John Bolton wrote in his book Trump was a traitor who tried to sell out his country to get China to help him win reelection. His own lawyer testified under oath that Trump paid hundreds of thousands of dollars in hush money to a Playboy Centerfold and a porn star. And you yourself said Trump was the dumbest white man you'd ever met. And now he's upset his niece says he paid someone to help him get into college?"

"That's it in a nutshell," said the Attorney General, getting into his side of the bed.

"Why, that just may be the nicest thing anyone's ever said about him."

"I'm afraid the President doesn't see it that way."

"Well, he certainly should," said his wife. "At least it shows he was smart enough to know how dumb he is."

And with that, William Barr's wife turned off the bedroom lights with a clap of her hands.

* * *

CHAPTER 12

"WHAT TANGLED WEBS WE WEAVE"

In the early morning hours of July 4 — 5:30 a.m. to be exact — Donald Trump Jr. was awakened by a phone call from his father, the President of the United States. Even before he could mumble "hello," Don Jr. was barraged by a tirade of venom:

"You fuckin' moron! You glorified errand boy! If it weren't for me, you'd be renting walk-up apartments in Spanish Harlem! You fuckin' imbecile!"

Don Jr. — for the life of him — could not figure out what he had done wrong. But his father was over-the-top mad. Mad even for Trump. Maybe not I'm-writing-you-out-of-the-will mad, but close.

His father went on: "Of all the fuckin' tweets you ever put out, this has got to be the stupidest, even for you. In the middle of an election, I don't have enough troubles with this virus thing from China, you got to tweet about Jeffrey Epstein! Just when I put that whole fuckin' mess behind me, you come along and stir it all up again. Moron! You got the fuckin' brains of your mother and she was an Einstein compared to you. You worthless piece of shit!"

When Trump paused to catch his breath, Don Jr. jumped in: "Pop, that tweet wasn't me. It came from Eric. He's the one who sent it. Not me."

"Well, don't fuckin' do it again," said Trump, hanging up.

Half asleep, Don Jr. reached across the bed for his girlfriend Kimberly Guilfoyle before realizing she wasn't there. She had tested positive for COVID-19 and was self-quarantining at her place. It would take another thirty minutes before Don Jr. fell back asleep.

At the White House, Trump saw no need to apologize. It was a natural mistake. Sometimes he couldn't tell one son from the other. Eric, Don Jr., Don Jr., Eric. The two Trump sons — often referred to behind their backs as Uday and Qusay (the nicknames Steve Bannon gave them after the sons of Saddam Hussein) — were to their father two fuck-ups from the same pod.

Eric Trump, the third child and second son of the President, was officially the co-executive of the Trump Organization and Senior Adviser to the President. Previously, he had been a boardroom judge on his father's TV show *The Apprentice* (twenty-three episodes) and, while still at Georgetown University, one of the judges for Trump's Miss Universe pageant. ("Isn't he tall and also first in his class" bragged Trump, introducing Eric to Miss Ecuador.)

Like his brother Don Jr., Eric was also a big-game hunter of endangered species. But of all the Trumps (except perhaps for the President himself), Eric was the most committed to conspiracy theories that warned of the evils of the "deep state" — those globalist elites devoted to destroying his father and his presidency.

The tweet the President was referring to was Eric's from July 3 which included a picture of former President Bill Clinton walking his daughter Chelsea down the aisle on her wedding day in 2010. Among the wedding guests pictured was Ghislaine Maxwell, former associate (and alleged procurer) of Jeffrey Epstein — the dead sex trafficker.

Eric Trump had written in the caption of the tweet "Birds of a Feather..."

Eric's tweet had been posted shortly after news of Maxwell's arrest by the FBI on charges of sexual abuse of minors. According to a grand jury indictment, Maxwell, acting as Epstein's accomplice, had recruited Epstein's underage victims. Accusations that Maxwell had denied.

(Author's note: At a press conference after her arrest, Trump — when asked about Ghislaine Maxwell — replied inexplicably: "I wish her well, frankly.")

Eric Trump's attempt to associate Bill Clinton with Maxwell created a firestorm response of anti-Trump tweets, which included pictures of President Trump partying with Maxwell and Epstein. For example:

> "Does the President's son not know there are photos of Donald Trump with Maxwell?"

and

> "Dear @EricTrump — here's one of a dozen photos of your father with Maxwell and Epstein. DOZENS across MANY YEARS"

Jeffrey Epstein and Donald Trump were once good pals, high-flying members of the New York social scene in the 1980s. Trump had described Epstein as a "fun guy" and "terrific person" and, in a *New York* magazine article in 2002, said of Epstein: "He is known to like beautiful women as much as I do, and many of them are on the younger side."

Epstein's problems with the law began in March 2005 when the Palm Beach Police Department received reports that Epstein had engaged in sexually inappropriate behavior with a minor. This began a thirteen-month undercover investigation of Epstein, which included a search of his home that produced a large number of photos of girls throughout the house. Details from the investigation included allegations that 12-year-old triplets were flown in from France for Epstein's birthday to be sexually abused by the financier.

After the Palm Beach Chief of Police requested assistance from the FBI, agents identified at least "thirty-four confirmed minors" whose allegations of sexual abuse by Epstein included corroborating details. The FBI investigation resulted in a fifty-three-page indictment in June 2007.

Coincidentally, it was in 2007 that Trump dropped Epstein socially, banning him from Mar-a-Lago where he had been a frequent guest.

Three prominent and well-connected lawyers represented Epstein in the case:

1) **Ken Starr**, the famous special prosecutor of Bill Clinton who nailed him on perjury in the Monica Lewinsky scandal;

2) **Roy Black**, the criminal attorney who represented William Kennedy Smith (rape), right-wing political talk show host Rush Limbaugh (drugs), and Joe Francis of *Girls Gone Wild* fame (child abuse and prostitution); and

3) **Alan Dershowitz**, Harvard law professor who once represented O.J. Simpson (double homicide).

Alan Dershowitz — noted scholar of Constitutional law — was, in a strange turn of events, himself named in a lawsuit by one of Epstein's victims, Virginia Roberts, who alleged in a sworn affidavit that at age 16 she had been sexually trafficked by Epstein and Ghislaine Maxwell for their own use and for use by several others, including Prince Andrew and retired Professor Dershowitz. Both Maxwell and Dershowitz denied the charges; Dershowitz even took legal action against her allegations. Dershowitz did admit, however, to having one massage at Epstein's New York mansion, but he says it was given by an old Russian woman and he kept his boxer shorts on the whole time.

The Professor also served as one of Trump's attorneys during the President's impeachment trial in the Senate.

Despite the serious allegations against Epstein in 2007, his lawyers were able to negotiate a Non-Prosecution Agreement with **Alexander Acosta**, then the U.S. attorney for the Southern District of Florida. Acosta agreed to a plea deal, granting Epstein immunity from all federal criminal charges, along with four named co-conspirators and other unnamed "potential co-conspirators." That agreement essentially shut down an ongoing FBI probe into whether there were more victims and other powerful people who took part in Epstein's sex crimes. At the time, this stopped the investigation and sealed the indictment.

The "sweetheart deal" that Acosta had agreed to allowed Epstein to plead guilty to a State Court charge, did not require him to register as a sex offender, and only had him serve a thirteen-month jail sentence, from which he was granted "work" release privileges of up to twelve hours a day to spend at home or in his office doing whatever he wanted.

Later, when pressed why he had agreed to the unbelievably lenient deal, Acosta said that he was told Epstein had very high connections in "Intelligence" and to "leave him alone."

It's not clear who it was who had told Acosta "better go easy," but other powerful people linked to Epstein and his trafficking in young girls allegedly included, but was not limited to, Bill Clinton (who strongly denied the charges), the aforementioned Alan Dershowitz, and Prince Andrew, who you would have thought as a member of the Royal Family and second son to Queen Elizabeth should have been able to get girls on his own.

As for Alexander Acosta: a former law clerk to conservative Supreme Court Justice Samuel Alito, Acosta, for some unknown reason, had always been highly regarded by Trump. *(Author's note: In fact, Acosta had been Trump's first choice for Attorney General.)* And in February 2017, Donald Trump announced that he would nominate Acosta to fill the position of Secretary of Labor. Acosta was confirmed by the U.S. Senate after receiving the support of all Republican Senators, and was sworn in by VP Mike Pence on April 28, 2017.

Ironically, one of Acosta's early proposals as Labor Secretary was to defund the International Labor Affairs Bureau, the agency that combats human trafficking, including child sex trafficking, from $68 million to under $20 million.

In November 2018, as Trump floated the idea of replacing then-AG Jeff Sessions with Acosta, the *Miami Herald* published an investigative report detailing Acosta's role in the Epstein case. That story revealed the extent of collaboration between Acosta and Epstein's influential attorneys in their efforts to keep victims from learning the terms of the plea deal, a violation of federal law.

On July 6, 2019, Epstein was arrested by the FBI-NYPD Crimes Against Children Task Force on sex trafficking charges stemming from activities alleged to have occurred between 2002 and 2005. A search of Epstein's Manhattan townhouse turned up new evidence of sex trafficking and also found "hundreds — and perhaps thousands — of sexually suggestive photographs of fully, or partially, nude females." Amid criticism of his mishandling of the Epstein case, Acosta resigned his role as Secretary of Labor effective July 19, 2019.

Epstein was found dead in his cell at the Metropolitan Correctional Center on August 10, 2019.

By the way, the Metropolitan Correctional Center is under the direct control of the Department of Justice, headed by now-Attorney General William Barr.

That is, of course, the same William Barr who, less than a year after Epstein's death, fired the U.S. Attorney for the Southern District of New York, longtime Republican Geoffrey Berman, who was investigating the Epstein case as well as those involving Trump's lawyer Rudy Giuliani. No reason given. Asked to comment on Berman's removal, Trump said: "We have a really capable Attorney General... I'm not involved."

One name missing, so far, in this complicated narrative is that of **Thomas Barrack**, a private real estate investor and founder and Executive Chairman of Colony

Capital Inc., which runs a $25 billion portfolio. Its North Star division has raised $7 billion since Trump became President, mostly from Saudi Arabia. Back in the 1990s, Barrack (now 73) played wingman to Jeffrey Epstein and Donald Trump as the Three Musketeers (as they were called) cut their way through New York's glamorous night life.

Unlike Trump, Barrack never officially denounced Epstein nor, as it seems, was ever asked to.

At present, Barrack, like other longtime Trump associates back in the day (Roger Stone would be another), remains one of Trump's most loyal supporters. Just how loyal can be demonstrated by the fact that in 2010 Barrack bought $70 million of Jared Kushner's debt on the Kushner-family-owned 666 Fifth Avenue building. Kushner later avoided bankruptcy when Barrack agreed to reduce his obligations after considerable massaging (figuratively speaking) by his buddy Donald Trump.

Barrack served as chairman of the Committee overseeing the Inauguration of

Donald Trump, which raised around $100 million (much still not accounted for) and was more than twice the amount spent on Obama's 2012 Inauguration. The Trump Committee's lavish spending included paying $3.6 million (or $450,000 per day) for the use of the ballroom at Trump's International DC Hotel. Eye-popping numbers that brought a lawsuit against the Committee for grossly overpaying for event space — money that went right into the pockets of the owners of the hotel: Trump, his daughter Ivanka, and sons Eric and Don Jr. Documents from that lawsuit revealed that all matters regarding entertainment had to be cleared by another Trump pal Steve Wynn, who himself was accused of sexual misconduct in 2018 and forced to resign as CEO of his casino companies and as Finance Chairman for the Republican National Committee.

In May 2019, Thomas Barrack came under investigation by the Eastern District of New York for not only his role as Chairman of the Inauguration Committee but his suspicious financial ties to the Middle East.

And while that investigation is still ongoing, reports released by a Congressional Committee revealed Barrack's plan to team up with Saudi Princes to buy a U.S. nuclear company — Westinghouse, a struggling manufacturer of nuclear reactors — and sell it, with as many as thirty nuclear reactors, to Saudi Arabia in a secret deal bypassing Congress, stoking fears that the kingdom was on its way to a nuclear bomb.

The report also suggested that Barrack used his extensive access to top administration officials, including Trump's Senior Adviser and son-in-law Jared Kushner, to advance the project that might mean billions to Barrack and his partners.

After Trump's blistering call to Don Jr., during which he had confused him, for good reason, with his brother Eric, the President went about his business. Rising from bed, he checked his Mike Lindell "GizaDreams" sheets — made from the world's best cotton grown only in a region between the Sahara Desert, the Mediterranean Sea, and the Nile River. Happily they were dry, sparing him the trouble of having to hide them from the housekeeping staff.

A quick shower, into his blue suit and red tie (scotch-taped together and fastened to his shirt to keep it from flapping loose) and Trump was ready for the day.

And what a day he had before him. It was Trump's July 4th Salute to America, which featured a luncheon on the South Lawn for staff, their family, friends, and Cabinet members; flyovers from all branches of the military; and a spectacular fireworks display following his televised remarks to the nation.

As he tied the laces on his Johnston & Murphy shoes — pausing to catch his reflection in the glossy black leather — he glanced down at a copy of the speech:

SPEECH TEXT

... my fellow Americans: the First Lady and I are delighted to welcome you to the second Salute to America...

... Two hundred and forty-four years ago in Philadelphia, the fifty-six signers of our Declaration of Independence pledged their lives, their fortunes, and their sacred honor to boldly proclaim this eternal truth: that we are all made equal by God...

... Thanks to the courage of those patriots of July 4th, 1776, the American Republic stands today as <u>the greatest, most exceptional, and most virtuous nation in the history of the world</u>...

* * *

CHAPTER 13

THE REPUBLICAN NATIONAL CONVENTION

It was July 11 when Trump met in the White House Situation Room for a briefing on plans for the Republican National Convention scheduled for August 24 to 27. Besides Trump, in attendance were Kellyanne Conway, Hope Hicks, Don Jr., Ivanka, and Jared Kushner.

The previous month, Trump had decided to move the Convention, originally scheduled for Charlotte, North Carolina, to Jacksonville, Florida when the Democratic governor Roy Cooper imposed a shelter-in-place order that would have severely limited the large, glitzy, made-for-television celebration that Trump demanded.

At the time, Florida had been one of only a handful of states that seemed to have had the spread of the coronavirus under control. But now, a month later, after Republican Governor

Ron DeSantis reopened the state, cases had spiked to record highs. Florida was now the epicenter of the epicenter, registering as many new cases per day as all of the European Union nations combined.

Undaunted, Trump assigned his most trusted advisers and family members to oversee the planning for the Jacksonville Convention, and it was today he was to hear their updated reports on the Convention's progress.

The following is an edited version taken from the official transcript of that meeting:

> Jared: Mr. President, I'd like to start by bringing you up to date on a few additional 'planks' that have been added to the 2020 platform as it now stands.
>
> The President: Sure.
>
> Jared: First — 'The Bible will be required reading in all public schools. Those schools not complying will be denied federal funding.'

The President: Good book, the Bible. My favorite. Right before *Art of the Deal*, which should also be required reading.

Jared: Second — 'Ground meats containing small particles of metal shall no longer be allowed to be recalled from grocery store shelves.'

The President: Makes sense to me.

Jared: Third — 'Chickens with minor infections may still be allowed to be labeled organic.'

The President: Perfect. These Obama regulations have been killing the poultry business.

Jared: Four — 'Gun owners diagnosed as criminally insane will have all their weapons returned to them immediately upon being released from their place of incarceration.'

Don Jr. And it's about time.

Jared: Five — 'Men who dress as women and women who dress as men are encouraged to use the bathroom before they leave the house.'

The President: Great. Terrific. What's next?

Kellyanne: Sir, we have designated the first night's theme to be 'Make the American Family Great Again.' The second night as 'Make American Streets Safe Again.' The third night — devoted to the economy — will be known as 'Make America Rich Again.' And the last night, the night of your acceptance speech: 'Make America Trump Again.'

The President: Like it. Good work.

Don Jr.: We have also prepared four fifteen-minute videos to be shown on each night in keeping with those themes. The first is called 'Sleepy Creepy Joe Biden.' The second 'The Terrorists on the Streets Are Coming to the Suburbs.' On the third night, we're repeating the video from 2016 that was very popular: 'Benghazi.' And on the last night, in your honor, the video is a series of clips we're calling 'President Trump's Biggest Hits,' a montage of your greatest accomplishments over the last four years.

<u>The President</u>: Don't forget to include 'And who's gonna pay for the virus? China!'

<u>Don Jr</u>.: Already in there.

<u>The President</u>: What about celebrities? We have to have celebrities. Movies. TV stars... Can't have a Convention without celebrities.

<u>Ivanka</u>: All covered. To start: Jon Voight.

The President: Great guy — Jon Voight. Never forget what he said about me after the Inauguration. Never forget it. He said, 'Abraham Lincoln is smiling today knowing America will be saved by an honest and good man who will work for all the people.' Cannot go wrong with Jon Voight.

Ivanka: Gary Busey has said yes.

The President: Amazing that Gary Busey. I fired him from *The Apprentice* — I think maybe the second week — and he still loves me. That's loyalty. Good for him.

Ivanka: We also contacted Scott Baio...

The President: *(interrupting)* Love that Scott Baio. Great speech he gave in 2016. What did he say? Something about me being the Messiah.

Don Jr.: He said you may not be the Messiah, but you're just the man who 'wants to give back to his country, America, the country that has given him everything'.

The President: *(disappointed)* Oh. Well, still pretty good. Love that Scott Baio.

Ivanka: Only problem is he doesn't want to fly commercial and he's asked we provide a private jet for him and his family.

The President: Fuck him. Who does he think he is? Hasn't had a hit since *Joanie Loves Chachi*.

Ivanka: I'll get back to him and see what we can work out.

The President: What about Jimmy Dean? Everybody loves Jimmy Dean.

Don Jr.: He's dead.

The President: Not James Dean. Everyone knows James Dean is dead. Killed in that car crash in the Fifties, for Godsakes.

Don Jr.: No, I mean Jimmy Dean. He's dead too.

The President: I saw him on a pork sausage commercial just the other day.

Don Jr.: No, Pop, I swear, Jimmy Dean's dead.

The President: Oh, I guess they musta made that commercial before he died.

Ivanka: Roseanne Barr is committed, but wants us to pick up her hotel accommodations.

The President: Fine. Put her up at the DoubleTree. But no room service. I've seen how she eats.

Ivanka: And also a 'yes' from Hulk Hogan, only he wants to know do you want him in a suit or his wrestling thong. He's not sure anyone will recognize him in a suit.

The President: A suit. But keep the headband.

Ivanka: We also have a 'yes' from Tila Tequila.

The President: Who?

Don Jr.: You remember her, Pop. She was in those reality shows *Big Brother* and *Pants-off Dance-Off*, and she sang on the MTV Video Music Awards show.

Ivanka: She would like to plug her new single 'Dialing While Drunk'.

Jared: I heard she got into some trouble posting pro-Hitler tweets.

The President: Better check that out. Don't want to hear from the 'Politically Correct People' about that. You know them and Hitler.

Ivanka: We also have RSVPs from Mike Tyson, Dennis Rodman, Kelsey Grammer, Willie Robertson from *Duck Dynasty,* Mike Ditka, and Bobby Knight, who said he thought it'd be funny if he threw a chair at a cutout of Joe Biden.

The President: Let me think about that.

Ivanka: I also have firm commitments from Steve Baldwin, Joey Travolta, and Frank Stallone.

The President: What about music? We need music...

Hope Hicks: We've lined up the singers for the National Anthem. The first night we have Kid Rock. The second night, Gene Simmons and KISS.

The President: In makeup or not? Because without makeup, they're all pretty ugly.

Hope Hicks: I'll make sure they're in makeup. On the third night, we have Ted Nugent, and on your night — the last night — we have The Mormon Tabernacle Choir.

The President: Powerful. Very powerful.

Hope Hicks: There's only one problem. Two hundred seventy-five members have tested positive to the coronavirus and seventy-one are in quarantine, so that leaves only four singers in the choir.

The President: Then we can call them The Mormon Tabernacle Quartet.

Hope Hicks, Jared, Ivanka, Kellyanne, & Don Jr.: *(together)* Great idea... Fantastic... Brilliant... Terrific... Wow...

The President: *(proudly)* That's why they pay me the big bucks.

Growing restless, the President adjourned the meeting ten minutes later with such issues as venues, security, hotel deposits, and the need for masks and social distancing still unresolved.

— End of Transcript —

With COVID cases in Florida up 1,500% in May, on July 25 the President announced he was cancelling the Republican National Convention in Jacksonville — "for the good of the country."

* * *

CHAPTER 14

TRUMP'S PHOTO OP AT THE NRA

With the press corps in tow, Donald Trump and Don Jr. arrived at the National Rifle Association headquarters — a vast, sky-blue, glass, sleek edifice in Fairfax, Virginia — on August 5, 2020. There was more to the visit, as it would turn out, than merely a series of publicity photos.

Trump and his son were met at the entrance by Executive Vice President Wayne LaPierre; Executive Director of the NRA's lobbying branch, Chris Cox; President Carolyn Meadows; and Honorary Chairman Chuck Norris — famous for his Total Gym (purchasable in monthly payments of $99.95) workout infomercial.

They were soon joined by Eddie Eagle, the adorable, fuzzy mascot with the large yellow beak, the namesake character developed by the NRA as the symbol for their children's programs promoting gun use for kids 5 through 12.

From the beginning of Trump's candidacy — even before he was nominated in 2016 — the NRA had endorsed Trump for President. Over the period of that campaign, the NRA spent more than $30 million in support of Trump, three times what it had ever spent on any other Presidential candidate.

Little known — as it was buried in the unread Mueller Report — was the charge that the Deputy Governor of the Central Bank of Russia, Aleksandr Torshin, had illegally funneled millions through the NRA to support Trump in 2016.

By the way, Torshin — a Russian Nationalist — was also a lifetime member of the NRA and close friend of President Vladimir Putin.

After posing for the cameras, Trump, Trump Jr., Cox, Carolyn Meadows, and LaPierre met privately in the NRA's 5th-floor boardroom. A meeting whose subject could have easily been titled "What can we do for each other lately?"

Aware of the President's limited attention span, Cox succinctly outlined NRA strategy in regard to the policy of "open carry" — the practice of openly carrying a firearm in public. At present, he told the President, there were twenty-six permissive carrying states — that is, states that did not require a permit or license to carry a gun on foot or in a motor vehicle.

"Great," interjected Trump.

"Trouble is," continued Cox, "there are twenty-four states and four territories with restrictions, including laws that forbid gun owners to 'open carry' when traveling from their state to those with restrictions. For example, Florida to New York."

"Not fair," said Trump.

"Our point exactly. Which is why our goal is to legislate those unfair gun laws all the way to the Supreme Court."

"And how can we help?" asked Don Jr.

"In three ways," said Carolyn Meadows. "First, of course, keep appointing conservative judges to the Supreme Court."

"Goes without saying," said Trump.

"Second, we'd like you to include a plank in the Republican platform stating our aims. We thought we'd write one up and send it to you for your approval."

"Not a problem," said Trump, who couldn't care less what was in his party's platform since he didn't know what was in it anyway.

"And lastly, we'd hope you could make 'open carry' an important feature at your rallies and press conferences. You know, as a part of your defense of the Second Amendment — that it's not enough to protect our guns, but it's the right of every citizen to be able to carry them, concealed or not, in public, especially during these perilous times of rioting and looting."

"After all, Mr. President," said Cox, "only you stand in the way between those who'd take our guns from us and our sacred Second Amendment rights as enshrined in the Constitution."

"We're down with that," said Don Jr. brightly, after a side glance at his father to see if he was still paying attention.

Donald Trump removed a folded sheet of white paper from his inside pocket. He placed it squarely in front of him and, without looking down, tapped it with his left hand. "I've got numbers here that say you guys are well below your last year's donations." He sat back in his chair, hugging his chest with both arms. You did not have to be an expert in body language to know the President meant business.

The move flustered the NRA people. Cox was the first to fill the awkward silence. "I believe we've spent over $15 million so far, Mr. President."

"It's going to take more than that," Trump said.

"I'm sure we can do something," said LaPierre to Cox.

"Good," said Trump. "And I need you to light some fires under Remington; Browning; Sturm, Ruger & Co.; Savage Arms; Springfield;

and Smith & Wesson. They're way behind where they should be."

Don Jr. marveled to himself how his father — not known for his memory — had recalled all the major gun manufacturers in the country.

"I think we can do that," said Cox affably.

"Good. I was thinking 20 to 40 mil all in by October," said Trump.

"Understood, sir," said LaPierre, with Cox and Carolyn Meadows nodding in agreement.

"Great," said Trump, "you can stay in touch with Don here. Anything you need, he's here to help."

Trump put the folded piece of paper back in his pocket. There was never any reason to look at it again because there was nothing written on it.

The rest of the day was, you could say, ceremonial. One photo op after the other:

Trump waved at, but did not get near, workers in the employee cafeteria.

At lunch in the executive dining room, Trump was presented with a specially made Smith & Wesson M&P 9mm handgun (retail price: $599) — the "American cop's favorite weapon" — with "Trump" engraved on the pearl handle, along with an alligator-skin holster, also with his name on it.

Next, with cameras rolling, Trump and Don Jr. were shown the NRA's family-friendly indoor shooting facility. There, under the direction of a professional instructor, Trump — outfitted in goggles and earplugs — was given a variety of weapons to try. Among them: a Lee-Enfield bolt-action rifle; an M16 self-loading rifle; a Soviet Union submachine gun; and a Glock 17 self-loading pistol.

> Trump was then presented with the standard NRA gag gift for visiting dignitaries: a paper target — with his name on it — showing six direct hits into the middle of the bull's-eye.

Afterwards, press and photographers accompanied Trump and son as they toured the NRA's National Firearms Museum (15,000 square feet) — a chronological history of 2,500 firearms over seven centuries, including a wheellock carbine brought over on the Mayflower; guns owned by Presidents Theodore Roosevelt, John F. Kennedy, and Ronald Reagan; and even Napoleon Bonaparte's flintlock fowler.

What the press and video cameras were not allowed to see was the NRA's private collection: firearms purchased by the NRA via front men (ostensibly to keep them out of the "wrong hands") — from private owners and at auction — of guns used in some of America's most infamous crimes.

Trump was one of the few ever — outside the NRA's most inner circle — to view the collection. To name a few of the weapons:

2017 LAS VEGAS SHOOTING — 58 DEAD — Semiautomatic rifles (with bump stocks), bolt-action rifle, revolver;

2016 ORLANDO NIGHTCLUB SHOOTING — 49 DEAD — Semiautomatic rifle and pistol;

2007 VIRGINIA TECH SHOOTING — 32 DEAD — Semiautomatic pistols;

1990 COLUMBINE HIGH SCHOOL MASSACRE — 13 DEAD — Semiautomatic carbine, shotguns, semiautomatic pistols;

2012 SANDY HOOK ELEMENTARY SCHOOL SHOOTING — 27 DEAD — Semiautomatic rifle and pistol;

And one of the most prized: The KelTec PF9 9mm handgun used by George Zimmerman to kill Trayvon Martin in 2012. Sold at auction to a "John Smith" for $250,000.

* * *

CHAPTER 15

THE VACCINE SCANDAL

At 5:45 p.m., Wednesday, September 9, the phone rang in the office of Trump's Chief of Staff Mark Meadows. It was Peter Baker, Chief White House Correspondent of *The New York Times*. Baker got right to the point: *The Times* was about to run a front-page story concerning a phone call Trump had made to the Director of the Center for Drug Evaluation and Research (CDER) at the Food and Drug Administration on July 31, 2020.

In essence, the story went like this: A whistleblower complaint — that was now in the hands of the Inspector General at the FDA — charged that the President had called the Director at CDER and, in asking for an update on the progress of a vaccine for coronavirus, had suggested that the Director could, in return for a quick approval, share in what were certain to be the vaccine's enormous profits.

Now in Phase 3, the vaccine was identified as a whole virus vaccine that used a weakened or inactivated version of the coronavirus to provoke an immune response and was the product of Superba Labs.

The CEO of Superba Labs, located in Boca Raton, Florida, had been a frequent guest at the White House and Mar-a-Lago and a longtime Republican donor to various Trump super PACs. Among one of the top recipients was the American People Committee, which received over $2.5 million in the last six months.

The story also noted that President Trump, who had labeled the search for a vaccine "Operation Warp Speed," had promised in tweets and at political rallies that a cure for the deadly disease was "just around the corner."

After Baker finished reading the rest of the story, Meadows took a deep breath and said: "Sounds very flimsy to me." Even Meadows knew he didn't sound convincing.

Baker: "We have three sources at FDA, not including the whistleblower's attorney, and we have the whistleblower's contemporaneous notes taken at the time of the President's call. We think it's only fair to give you guys a chance to comment. Either way, we're going with what we got."

"How much time do I have?" asked Meadows, the blood still draining from his face.

"Two hours," said Baker flatly.

Meadows personally retrieved the White House record of Trump's July 31 call from what was known as the TNet System, the top-secret-level computer network that connects with the executive branch's top-secret network called JWICS.

Meadows was shocked by what he read: a phone conversation — not very long — between Trump and the Director of Drug Evaluation and Research, from the Oval Office and obviously when Meadows was not present.

Meadows immediately called Hope Hicks. When there was bad news for the President, it always helped to have Hope Hicks by your side. Hicks was the longtime personal assistant to the President — and looked on by Trump as a second daughter. She could always be counted on to soothe and comfort the President no matter how desperate and dark things might seem. And if there was ever a time Meadows needed Hope Hicks, it was now.

Brought up to date, Hicks with Meadows made the short walk to the Oval Office.

Meadows was certain that Trump would "rip his face off" (as the common expression went around the West Wing) for bringing him bad news right before his dinner. But Hope Hicks was not so sure. Years of working with Trump taught her one thing: no matter the situation, no matter how good or bad, Trump was consistently unpredictable.

She remembered the night four years ago during the 2016 campaign at a Marriott outside Canton, Ohio when she was in bed with Corey Lewandowski, her boyfriend at the time — and the pillow talk turned to their boss and what it was that made him such a puzzle, even to those who had known him since his early real estate days in New York.

Corey had said that one piece of the puzzle had to be Trump's severe Attention Deficit Disorder (ADD), an inability to focus on any one thing for more than a minute. Corey had put it this way: "I think there are times that he doesn't even know he didn't get laid."

Hope remembered that line as the only clever thing Corey Lewandowski ever said.

Trump was just getting off a call when Meadows and Hicks entered the open door of the Oval Office. "Don't bullshit a bullshitter," they heard the President say before hanging up.

Meadows quickly ran down the situation, beginning with the telephone call from Baker at *The New York Times*. Trump listened impassively. Then Hope Hicks handed Trump the transcript of his July 31 call.

"Yeah," the President said, "I remember this. And what's wrong with it? It was a perfect call."

"I know," said Hope Hicks delicately, "but it could be interpreted differently."

Trump went on: "What I said in this phone call is perfectly stated. This is just another media hoax to hand the election to the Democrats."

"We need to respond to *The Times,"* said Meadows.

"Tell them that this whistleblower is an obviously disgruntled Obama holdover who has deliberately misinterpreted what I said. All I was doing was making sure we didn't fall behind the Chinese in coming up with a cure for the virus."

"Very good, sir," agreed Meadows, "and we can also say that this whistleblower should be criminally charged for leaking classified information."

"Great," said Trump, "and call Barr at Justice and tell him I want a full investigation."

"The only problem is," said Hope Hicks, "there is more than one person who heard this call and that could prove, well, problematic if the Democrats in the House call for a full investigation."

"Then release the transcript of the call," said Trump.

Meadows and Hope Hicks exchanged looks, both thinking the same thing: the transcript did not only not exnerate the President but, in fact, showed him making an effort to pressure the FDA to approve a COVID-19 vaccine regardless of its efficacy.

"Sir, I'm not sure that's a good idea," said Hope Hicks.

"I don't give a shit what you think," Trump said politely. "It couldn't have been a better call. It proves I was acting on behalf of the American people like a President should. Release the goddamn transcript. That'll put an end to it right then and there."

Trump picked up his cell phone, about to make a call, signaling the meeting was over.

Back in his office, Meadows — ashy and solemn — called Baker at *The Times,* claiming the whistleblower's complaint had mischaracterized the President's phone call to the FDA and, to support that claim, the White

House would be releasing a redacted version of the call by tomorrow — once it was declassified.

Hiding his surprise, Baker thanked Meadows for the statement.

The next morning, the following transcript was posted on the President's Facebook page, September 10, 2020:

~~SECRET//ORCON/NOFORN~~

[PkgNumberShort]

UNCLASSIFIED

Declassified by order of the President
September 10, 2020

~~EYES ONLY~~
~~DO NOT COPY~~

MEMORANDUM OF TELEPHONE CONVERSATION

SUBJECT: ~~(C)~~ Telephone Conversation with Director for Drug Evaluation and Research

PARTICIPANTS: Dr. XXX

Notetakers: The White House Situation Room

DATE, TIME AND PLACE: July 31, 2020, 9:03-9:07 a.m. EDT Residence

(TEXT STARTS NEXT PAGE)

CAUTION: A Memorandum of a Telephone Conversation (TELCON) is not a verbatim transcript of a discussion. The text in this document records the notes and recollections of Situation Room Duty Officers and NSC policy staff assigned to listen and memorialize the conversation in written form as the conversation takes place. A number of factors can affect the accuracy of the record, including poor telecommunications connections and variations in accent and/or interpretation. The word "inaudible" is used to indicate portions of a conversation that the notetaker was unable to hear.

Classified By: 2354726
Derived From: NSC SCG
Declassified On: 20441231

UNCLASSIFIED

~~SECRET//ORCON/NOFORN~~

~~SECRET//ORCON/NOFORN~~

2

UNCLASSIFIED

~~(S/NF)~~ The President: Doctor, good morning. Good to meet you. Heard lots of good things about you. Dr. Fauci told me you were the main guy to talk to when it came to my Operation Warp Speed. So, tell me, how's it looking?

~~(S/NF)~~ Dr. XXX: Good morning, Mr. President. And I think I can say we're making excellent progress.

~~(S/NF)~~ The President: Good to hear. I was hoping you could update me on that Superba Labs vaccine. My friends there tell me that they haven't heard from you in a while.

~~(S/NF)~~ Dr. XXX: Well, sir. We're doing the best we can.

~~(S/NF)~~ The President: You know, the Chinese are already testing half their goddamn army. It'd sure look bad if the Chinese -- who started the virus -- end up coming up with a cure before we do.

~~(S/NF)~~ Dr. XXX: I understand, sir. And I can assure you we're doing everything we can to make sure that doesn't happen.

UNCLASSIFIED

~~SECRET//ORCON/NOFORN~~

~~(S/NF)~~ The President: So, where are we exactly on this -- on the Superba thing?

~~(S/NF)~~ Dr. XXX: Well, Mr. President, I'd hate to get too far out in front of our data, but let's just say we're getting closer to a final evaluation every day.

~~(S/NF)~~ The President: We got lots of Americans counting on you.

~~(S/NF)~~ Dr. XXX: I know that, sir.

~~(S/NF)~~ The President: Anyway, my friends at Superba wanted me to let you know they're willing to do whatever it takes. And regarding that, they ran some numbers by me which I think you'll find very interesting. They told me that, based on what is being charged for a vial of Remdesivir, which I'm told is $300 a vial, a vaccine that immunized the world's population against COVID-19 could probably cost at least the same, which means when you multiply that by a million vials a year, we're talking at least about 100 billion... that's 'b' for billion... dollars a year. And that's just for one year and that doesn't really cover half the country. So, let's say, you were to

UNCLASSIFIED

get 1% of that -- that would mean you could walk away when this is all done with what?, hundreds of millions for yourself and anybody else you wanted...

~~(S/NF)~~ Dr. XXX: I'm not sure how to respond to that, Mr. President.

~~(S/NF)~~ The President: That's okay. Just want to put that out there. You know -- as they say -- 'one hand washes the other'. Just something to keep in mind. I would be very grateful. My friends at Superba would also be very grateful, not to mention the American people.

~~(S/NF)~~ Dr. XXX: (INAUDIBLE)

~~(S/NF)~~ The President: And just to follow up, I'm going to have my lawyer Rudy Giuliani -- I know you've heard of him -- highly respected guy -- call you and, you know, see how we can move things along before October at the latest.

~~(S/NF)~~ Dr. XXX: Yes, sir.

~~(S/NF)~~ The President: Great, really great talking to you.

~~(S/NF)~~ Dr. XXX: Thank you for calling, Mr. President. Bye-bye.

-- End of Conversation --

CHAPTER 16

REACTIONS FROM REPUBLICAN SENATORS

The day after the September 10 transcript was released to the press, Paula Reid, CBS White House Correspondent, stood just south of the Rotunda in the Capitol Building — a few feet in front of the statue of Jefferson Davis — trying to get passing Republican Senators to comment on the President's phone call to the FDA in which it appeared Trump was offering a bribe in order to get a quick approval of the COVID-19 vaccine manufactured by Superba Labs.

MS. REID

(to Senator Susan Collins of Maine:)

Senator Collins, would you comment on the transcript of the President's call?

SENATOR COLLINS

I'm sorry. I didn't read the full transcript and I never comment on anything I haven't read as yet.

(the Senator exits)

MS. REID

(to Senator Lindsey Graham of South Carolina:)

Senator, your reaction to the President's 'vaccine' transcript?

SENATOR GRAHAM

Seems like a perfectly reasonable request for the President of the United States to want to incentivize a cure for a terrible disease ravaging our nation. Trump wants to save America. Democrats want to end it.

(the Senator exits)

MS. REID

(to Senator Mitch McConnell
of Kentucky:)

Senator McConnell, would you
care to —

SENATOR McCONNELL

I'm sorry. I'm late for lunch.

(the Senator exits)

* * *

CHAPTER 17

TRUMP PREPS FOR THE FIRST DEBATE

It was a great day for golf. The weather was warm. The sun was out, its rays filtered through passing clouds, and the cooling breeze was slight enough not to change the course of the ball. All the more reason Trump was irate that he had agreed to spend the day preparing for the upcoming debate — scheduled for September 29 between him and his Democratic rival.

Unlike previous debates, these three were to be moderated by a single news anchor per debate. The first (and already announced) was to be Fox's Chris Wallace in a ninety-minute format with no interruptions.

Since mid-August, Jared Kushner, concerned by the President's lagging poll numbers, had tried to convince Trump he needed an intense seventy-two hours of preparation if he were to score the early knockout necessary to pull closer in the race, especially in the swing states Trump had won in 2016.

Kushner's plan was to convert a conference room in the White House into a smaller version of a debate stage: lecterns, a Biden stand-in, Jared himself playing Chris Wallace, and selected Senior Staff Advisers as members of the audience — Hope Hicks, Ivanka, and Stephen Miller — to critique Trump's performance.

Trump was opposed. "No fuckin' way," he explained.

There were several reasons for Trump's resistance: Trump always hated rehearsals, preferring his improvised skills, his on-the-spot gut responses, to memorized and stilted answers. Besides, he hated being judged, then coached, especially by women.

What Trump proposed instead was a weekend at his Trump National Golf Club in Bedminster, New Jersey. Bedminster had been his "lucky" site where he had prepped for the

2016 debates against Hillary Clinton and there was no reason this time to do it any differently.

In fact, Trump told Kushner he wanted Chris Christie to supervise the briefing, just as he had done four years ago.

It was a deliberate choice that Trump knew would annoy his son-in-law since it was Christie, in 2005, who had been the prosecutor to send Kushner's father Charles to federal prison for fourteen months for tax evasion, illegal campaign contributions, and witness tampering. Just another way Trump had of letting his son-in-law know he was still angry with him because he wore a mask to a coronavirus briefing.

Trump also suggested Jason Miller, who had just joined the campaign as a high-level strategist, to play Biden. Jason Miller was not one of Jared's favorite people. After the 2016 election, Miller was announced as Trump's choice for White House Communications Director, but had to withdraw when it became known that the married Miller had had an extramarital affair with a campaign staffer named A.J. Delgado, who later bore his illegitimate child. (Miller was also accused by Ms. Delgado of having impregnated a stripper, afterwards secretly administrating an abortion pill to this unnamed woman. Miller denied the charges, suing the mother of his child for $100 million in a defamation suit that went nowhere.)

Jared, however, Trump said, could still play Chris Wallace.

A few facts about the Bedminster Golf Club:

Trump bought the 530-acre property from the bankrupt estate of John DeLorean for $35 million in 2002. *(Author's note: DeLorean is famous for having been arrested in 1982 for cocaine trafficking. He was acquitted when a jury believed he was set up by the FBI. His car, the DeLorean — with its gull wings — was featured in the movie* Back to the Future.*)*

Members pay an initiation fee of $300,000. At a lunch, Trump told the assembled members that "This is my real group. You are my special people." The New Jersey tax bill for Bedminster was reduced from $90,000 to $1,000 after Trump grew hay on the property and kept nine goats in order to meet the state's agricultural requirements.

In 2015, Trump recorded plans to build a family cemetery on the grounds, including a large marble mausoleum for himself. "Who wouldn't want to be buried here?" he said one day, looking down at the 18th hole.

Precisely at noon, September 17, Jared Kushner arrived outside Trump's villa at Bedminster where he and Ivanka had a cottage on the grounds. Jared wore a Gucci polo shirt (retail $780) and color-coordinated, Gucci-striped leather track pants (retail $3,950), looking leaner and whiter than usual — like a walking marshmallow.

A few minutes later, Chris Christie arrived, already working up a sweat, tieless, dressed for business, and carrying a briefing book the size of the old Manhattan Yellow Pages.

Jason Miller was not far behind, holding an accordion folder with flash cards, reams of research, and multicolored bullet points assembled under topics like the economy, immigration, and the pandemic.

Fifteen minutes later, Trump — in full golf attire — emerged from his private villa — actually, a two-level condo with a balcony. Without "hellos," he motioned that they all sit at a wrought-iron table by the pool. Hovering in the background were the Secret Service dressed in Country Club Casual.

After Trump ordered out for two large 16" pizzas — meatballs, no cheese — from his favorite pizzeria, Bedminster Pizza, the four got to work.

Jared, as Chris Wallace, posed the first question: "Congress has passed a bipartisan bill that includes removing the names of military bases named after Confederate Generals — Ft. Hood, Ft. Benning, and Ft. Bragg. Why are you opposed?"

Trump didn't have to pause to think: "As President, I will continue to defend our great, really great American history against the angry mobs, directed by radical leftists, to destroy and defame our most sacred heritage. Our great American soldiers have trained at those forts. Their names carry hundreds of years of American military greatness. And I won't let it happen. Just like they want to tear down statues of our terrific heroes like President Andrew Jackson, Christopher Columbus, and Jesus. Not going to happen as long as I'm President. <u>Now</u> these same Marxist radicals have gotten them to change the name of the Washington Redskins. What's next — Tonto? Where would The Lone Ranger be without his Tonto? Or Red Ryder without his Little Beaver? And what about Chief Wahoo, beloved mascot of the Cleveland Indians? Is he next? And what about the Atlanta Braves — are they going to have to change their name too? I'm not a Braves fan myself, but I will protect their right to do the Tomahawk Chop as long as I'm President."

Before Jared could turn to Jason Miller to respond as Biden, Chris Christie interrupted: "Mr. President, if I may, I'm not sure you want to defend Andrew Jackson since he was responsible for the deaths of over hundreds of thousands of Native Americans when he took their lands and forcibly marched them out of the South thousands of miles away to the western part of the country."

"Then why'd they put him on the $20 bill if he was so terrible?"

"Well, that's why they want to take him off," answered Christie.

"Not while I'm around," snapped Trump. "Next question."

"VP Biden, your response," said Jared.

"Fuck Biden. Whatever he says is bullshit anyway. Next question," said Trump.

Jared consulted his cards, then asked: "Mr. President, there have been reports in the media that suggested if you were to lose the election you may not concede to the winner."

"Sure," said Trump, "I'll concede as long as it's a fair-and-square election. But if there's what I think will happen, if there's widespread election fraud... especially with the mail-in votes... well, then, I'll just have to make up my mind."

"VP Biden, your answer to that?"

Jason Miller as Biden replied: "Well, I find that very troubling. Since the peaceful transition of power in this country has always been one of our nation's most sacred traditions."

"Yeah, well, stealing an election is also a Democrat tradition and so what I'm saying now is I'll just keep you in suspense, okay?"

Kushner/Wallace continued: "Mr. President, given the pandemic, many Americans are concerned about their health insurance. Can you lay out your plan for health care if you're reelected?"

Trump: "This is an important subject. But there are lots of important subjects. Maybe it's in the Top 10 of subjects. Probably is. But there's heavy competition for the Top 10. So you can't be certain for sure, could be Top 12, Top 15. But certainly in the Top 20."

Trump stopped there either because he thought he had answered the question or because the pizzas had arrived.

"Dig in," said Trump. "Best pizza in New Jersey."

While they ate, Kushner/Wallace asked his next question: "Sir, every president since Nixon has released his tax returns. Why not you?"

"Because I'm still under audit. That's why."

Jason Miller leaned forward and, in hushed tones, said: "Mr. President, I have contacts at *The New York Times*. There's a rumor they've gotten access to your last ten years of tax returns that show, among other things, that you've only paid $750 a year since you've been President. They plan on breaking the story before the first debate."

"Fuck the failing *New York Times*," said Trump. "Who do you think my people are going to believe — me or their own eyes?"

Kushner tensed, remembering the $72 million refund Trump got a few years ago, then asked as Wallace: "Sir, when Obama was President, he paid more than $1 million in taxes, yet you've only paid $750 a year. Can you respond?"

"Yeah, because Obama's stupid and I'm a brilliant businessman," said Trump, his mouth crammed with pizza.

Before Kushner could get to his next question, Trump spotted one of Bedminster's more famous members, Joe Torre, ex-manager of the New York Yankees, L.A. Dodgers, and now Special Assistant to the Commissioner of Baseball.

"Joe!" Trump shouted.

"Didn't mean to interrupt, Mr. President," said Torre as he approached. "Just wanted to come by and say hello."

"Not at all," said Trump. "Pull up a chair and join us. Have some pizza."

Joe Torre sat. "This is the great Yankee manager Joe Torre," said Trump. "And this is my son-in-law Jared, and this is one of my most important strategists, Jason Miller. And I'm sure you know Chris Christie — could've been President of the United States if he hadn't hugged Obama."

Awkward laughter all around as the men bumped elbows.

"Looks like you've already got a round in," said Trump.

"Barely broke 90," Joe replied.

"Old or new course?" asked Trump, starting on his second slice of pizza, leaving the crust as was his custom.

"The new. And I have to say, Mr. President, it's a fantastic course. Except, please, that 4th hole — 560 yards, par 5? Kills me every time."

"That's why I put in those forward tees, gives you a chance to get the ball really out there."

"And the 14th is murder. Never yet missed one of those bunkers."

After another slice, Trump turned to Torre to ask: "Think you can go around round?"

"When?"

"Right now. I'm not doing anything."

"Well..."

"What's your handicap?"

"6.5."

"Mine's 2.6," said Trump. *(Author's note: Jack Nicklaus is a 3.7.)* "Play you fifty bucks a hole."

"Promise you'll go easy on me, Mr. President."

"I play to win — just so you know."

Torre, who had been a member at Bedminster for years, had never played with the President, so it was hard to turn him down.

Besides, he had heard all the stories that Trump was one of golf's greatest cheaters (the caddies called Trump "Pelé", after the great soccer legend, because he was always kicking the ball out of the bunkers). Torre was curious to see for himself.

As Torre and Trump stood, Kushner asked hopefully: "Maybe we can do a session later today?"

"I don't need any more sessions. I know all the answers. It's simple. Black and white. We're American. And they're not." With that, Trump and Torre walked off toward the clubhouse.

"You know I'm the Club champion," they all heard Trump say before the two disappeared from sight.

Christie could not help but be reminded of the story of Kim Jong-un, the North Korean dictator, who had boasted of having shot eighteen hole-in-ones on his first day playing golf. And no one in North Korea ever dared to say he hadn't.

"I guess that does it for today," Christie said, putting away his briefing book. Miller his flash cards.

Kushner was soon left alone at the table, looking down at a page of jokes he had never gotten to show the President. They were from Dennis Miller by way of Tucker Carlson. Mostly "Biden-is-so-old" zingers. The first one read "Biden always wears a mask because he forgot where he put his dentures."

There were ten more one-liners just as clever, but what good were they? Trump would never use them. His hopes of becoming Secretary of State fading fast, Jared sat staring forlornly into space as pigeons circled at his feet, pecking at the pellets of meatballs that had fallen from Donald Trump's lap.

The following day, after a rally in Bemidji, Minnesota, Trump was informed of Ruth Bader Ginsburg's death. Within the next few minutes, he got calls from Rudy Giuliani, Alan Dershowitz, and Jeanine Pirro, hinting that they'd like the job. Trump listened impassively, the smirk never leaving his lips.

* * *

CHAPTER 18

THE OCTOBER SURPRISE

Nobody could have guessed that the so-called "October Surprise" would be that President Trump (and the First Lady) would test positive for COVID-19.

After being outed by a Bloomberg reporter, Trump tweeted the news early Friday morning, October 2:

> "Tonight, @FLOTUS and I tested positive for COVID-19. We will begin our quarantine and recovery process immediately. We will get through this TOGETHER!"

Immediately, the left-wing media — led by CNN and MSNBC — connected the ironic dots: Proof of the President's reckless response to the virus; his super-spreader rallies; his ridicule of wearing masks; and that now the coronavirus had become the central issue of the 2020 campaign, all but dooming Trump's chance for reelection.

The liberal media also pointed out that Trump's recent prerecorded speech for the Alfred E. Smith Memorial Foundation Dinner in New York included his remarks that the country had finally turned the corner on the virus.

Fox News took a much different approach. Images of Trump always showed him wearing a mask. China was bashed for deliberately inventing the virus in a Wuhan lab. Tucker Carlson hinted slyly at an unknown conspiracy to infect the President with less than forty days before the election. Don Jr. appeared to assure the nation that his father was a warrior who would soon be back on the campaign trail. That was backed up by reports that the President was asymptomatic, in good spirits, and hard at work fulfilling his Presidential duties.

Fox's commentators reminded their audience all the President had done to combat the virus: The China ban; those mercy ships he sent to New York and Los Angeles; the abundance of ventilators he had produced; and his "warp-speed" program to manufacture a vaccine by election day.

By Friday morning, it was reported that the President — quarantined in his bedroom — was not only "resting comfortably" but was "quite energized."

As doctors administered various therapeutics — baby aspirin, zinc, Vitamin D, and some kind of experimental cocktail — Trump watched Fox News while fielding phone calls from well-wishers:

Senator Lindsey Graham called to tell Trump that his nominee for the Supreme Court was still right on course. "Hang in there, sir," kidded Graham, "and make sure Pence stays healthy. Or else we'll have ourselves a President Nancy Pelosi."

Trump failed to see the humor.

Vladimir Putin called from Moscow and wished the President a speedy recovery, then added, "At least you weren't poisoned."

His old friend, Madagascar's President Andry Bajoelina, phoned to tell Trump he was sending him an herbal tea labeled "COVID Organics," an amber liquid made from ground periwinkle (a flowering plant of the Dogbanes family) that not only cured COVID-19 but diabetes, malaria, and stomach cancer. "It's even been said to grow hair," said the African dictator in all seriousness.

There was the long-distance call from Israel (reversing the charges) by Sara, Benjamin "Bibi" Netanyahu's wife, reminding the President to drink lots of chicken soup. "Also an enema wouldn't hurt," she said. "It may not help, but it couldn't hurt either."

Occasionally, Trump would look up at the TV screens to hear a discussion of his underlying conditions. "I'm not fuckin' obese!" he'd yell with as much strength as he could muster before nodding off.

Telegrams poured in by the thousands. Between naps, Trump managed to read a few:

"Remember, God cares about you and hears our prayers that you will be well soon."

The Proud Boys

and

"My Darling Dear Mr. President: Recover soon. I miss you so much, my heart aches from your absence. Your one and only — "

Kim Jong-un

It was not certain if those were the North Korean's exact words or merely a bad translation.

Later in the day, Trump developed a low-grade fever. Perhaps it was his temperature combined with all the Fox News he'd been watching that sent him, drifting, into a reverie in which he saw a hazy vision of the future:

His infection was not the end of his campaign but the beginning. Just as he had after his Atlantic City bankruptcies, he would arise stronger, more powerful, yes — even greater than ever before. He had met the Enemy and had survived. Not merely survived but conquered. Who could not love him now? A triumphant Savior risen from the dead. A war-time President — injured in battle — returning to the front, ready once again to lead his troops into battle for the soul of America.

His own cough woke him from his half sleep. At his bedside were his assembly of doctors. They had agreed, they told him, that it would be best — out of an abundance of caution — to move him to a hospital for more precise monitoring. Reluctantly and not a little spooked, Trump okayed the decision.

At 6:17 Friday night and under his own power, Trump entered the Marine One helicopter for the short flight to Walter Reed National Military Medical Center.

Within the week, the President had recovered enough to return to the White House. There he would continue to rest until the first opportunity appeared to show America he was his former and brilliant self.

That opportunity, surprisingly, would come soon enough.

* * *

CHAPTER 19

THE SECOND OCTOBER SURPRISE

Trump Tower is a 58-floor skyscraper at 721-725 Fifth Avenue between 56th and 57th Streets in Midtown Manhattan. It is what is called a mixed-use building with retail stores, offices, and residential units plus an atrium on the first floor.

In addition to the penthouse condominium — once the home of Donald Trump (before officially moving to Palm Beach) — the building serves as headquarters for the Trump Organization as well as the New York office for his campaign.

It was built by Trump starting in 1979 and completed in 1983 at a cost of $300 million. In 2013, its estimated mortgage was above $100 million.

In July 2020, New York Mayor Bill de Blasio had the words "Black Lives Matter" painted in yellow letters on Fifth Avenue directly in front of the building.

It was early Tuesday morning, October 20, at around 3:30 a.m. that a four-alarm fire broke out in the Trump Tower lobby, caused (as it turned out) by unknown arsonists who had thrown a crude incendiary device — a Molotov cocktail, perhaps — through the lobby's plate-glass doors. No one was injured and the New York City Fire Department was able to limit the damage to the lower floor.

Awakened by the news, Trump quickly tweeted his reaction: "MOB VIOLENCE STRIKES AGAIN!! TERRORISTS WILL PAY!!!"

Trump's mind quickly spun into action. He would use the "firebombing" to boost his sluggish campaign: a visit to his New York office to assess the damage would drive home in one photo op all the "law-and-order" themes he'd been wailing about since June.

Trump broke his plan in a phone call to Don Jr. "What's the damage?" Trump asked.

"Lobby's scorched black. But the elevators still work. Nobody's allowed in since it's been designated a crime scene."

"Don't let anyone clean it up. I want it left just the way it is."

"Sure, Pop, but why?"

"I'm thinking it'd be good to show up with the White House Press Corps and address the violence in our cities."

"Great idea, Pop. It'd be like Churchill visiting bomb sites in World War II."

"The only difference is Churchill never made a really great speech."

"And you know what else would be neat?" said Don Jr. "If you carried that gun the NRA gave you. You could talk about how you can carry it legally in Florida but not in New York. The guys at the NRA would love you for it. And I think we could get another couple million out of them."

"Well, you handle that part. I'm flying in tomorrow once I coordinate everything from this end. And remember — leave the lobby just the way it is. And not a word to anybody — I want this to be a surprise. My October surprise."

Melania was in her walk-in closet deciding on what to wear for her one o'clock lunch with the wives of some of her husband's biggest donors. There were ten women, married to the richest men in America and longtime Trump supporters who, at last year's event, had humorously called themselves "White Wives Matter." But that was, of course, before all the George Floyd ruckus.

White House staff had given Melania flash cards with each woman's name and their picture so Melania would know who was married to whom and what their favorite topics of conversation were.

With one hand holding a card with a picture of Miriam, the wife of Sheldon Adelson (owner of the Las Vegas Venetian and expected to donate over $200 million to the 2020 Trump campaign), Melania sorted through her wardrobe for just the perfect outfit, all the while repeating to herself: "Miriam Adelson — nickname Miri. Favorite subjects: Israel, marijuana abuse, and annexation of Palestine. Pet peeves: Muslims, Iranians, and waiters who interrupt when you are in the middle of a conversation."

Melania was deciding between an off-the-shoulder Alexander McQueen printed gown (retail $13,500) and an Emilia Wickstead pink crepe top and high-waisted skirt (retail $11,999) when Trump burst in. He was dressed for his trip to New York: dark blue suit, white shirt, and power red tie. Like his underwear, Trump only wore his shirts once (as was said about the comedian Jerry Lewis in his heyday).

"How do I look?" he asked, turning full circle.

"The same," Melania answered, her mind elsewhere.

"Do you think I look fat?"

"You always look fat," she said.

"Be serious," Trump said. "I'm wearing a bulletproof vest and I want to know if it makes me look fat."

"You think someone is going to shoot you?" asked Melania, holding a mauve Roksanda "Margot" dress ($9,500) up to her neck. "I hope you're still not using those steroids."

"I'm going to New York today to give a speech and the Secret Service is worried."

"That's all they do," she said, "is worry."

"I want to know: can you tell if I'm wearing a bulletproof vest?" Trump insisted.

"Yes, it does make you lumpier than usual," she said.

Now it was Trump who checked himself in the mirror and was not happy with what he saw. He about-faced and was on his way out when he picked out a $35,000 floral Dolce & Gabbana, handed it to her, and said, "You should wear this."

Trump took the flight of stairs down to his master bedroom. Melania was right. The bulletproof vest did make him look fat. He asked himself what Putin would do. Putin wouldn't be caught dead in a bulletproof vest. Trump ripped off the vest, then got an idea. Instead, he'd wear — as Don Jr. suggested — the holster with the Smith & Wesson M&P 9mm the NRA had given him. Maybe even let the press get a glimpse of it. Just to let everyone know the kind of tough he-man their President really was.

He opened a bottom drawer and took out the gun nestled in its alligator-skin shoulder holster, which he slipped on under his suit jacket. Admired himself in the mirror for a minute, then headed to the Oval Office. He could hear Marine One warming up on the South Lawn.

At 2:30 that afternoon, Trump arrived at the West Side Heliport where he was met by Don Jr. and various Senior Staff Advisers from the campaign. Father and son were taken by limousine, following a police escort, to Trump Tower.

Protesters in the hundreds lined the street opposite the building, held back by well-armed New York riot police. The White House Press

Corps, joined by media outlets from around the world, were already on the scene.

After a brief tour of the lobby where Trump posed inspecting the damage, he stepped out onto Fifth Avenue. Standing in front of a lectern with the Presidential Seal, and after adjusting the microphone, Trump addressed the TV cameras lined in front of him.

But no sooner were the words “My fellow Americans” out of his mouth when he was interrupted by the chants of protesters yelling “Black Lives Matter!” ... “No Justice, No Peace!” ... and “Fuck Trump!”

One protester wearing a T-shirt with “Dump the Turd on November 3rd” was dragged out of the crowd, handcuffed, and led off in a police van. Outraged by what appeared to be an unjustified arrest, the crowd pushed against the barricades. The cops — batons at the ready — struggled to control the surge of angry protesters.

Loud “pops” from firecrackers could be heard as they landed at the feet of the outmanned police force.

Trump looked out nervously toward the demonstrators toppling the barricades across the street as the alarmed Secret Service tried to push him into the President's limo where Don Jr. was inside waiting.

"Mr. President, this way!" yelled an Agent, grabbing Trump around the waist.

But Trump worried how it would look — fleeing fearfully from the scene — held his ground, and instead took out his Smith & Wesson 9mm and, like Randolph Scott in a "B" Western, aimed it in the general direction of the protesters.

Nobody could quite believe what happened next: the President pulled the trigger. The mainspring drove the hammer and the gun fired — a single shot! — into the crowd. A young white man in his 20s — wearing a black hoodie — fell, bleeding, onto the sidewalk.

Stunned Agents wrestled the gun from Trump's hand and hustled him into the limo, which sped off down Fifth towards the West Side and the waiting Marine One helicopter.

In the back seat of the limo, Trump's face had drained of all its orange. "What the hell happened?" he asked Don Jr.

"You shot a protester," said his son.

"Nobody told me the gun was loaded," said Trump, gasping for air.

"It's not a gun if it isn't loaded," said Don Jr.

The Agent in the front seat beside the driver got off his walkie-talkie: "The victim is conscious and in stable condition and is now in an ambulance on its way to ColumbiaDoctors on 51st."

Sweating from every pore of his 300-pound body, Trump managed a small sigh of relief.

"This is going to be great for us," said Don Jr.

Trump stared at his son in disbelief.

"Think about it. You defended yourself like any patriotic American would against an Antifa agitator who was about to attack you."

"Right. An Antifa agitator," said Trump mechanically. "That's the ticket."

"Boy, is the NRA gonna love this," said Don Jr.

Within minutes, the President and Don Jr. had arrived at the West Side Heliport and were back in the White House forty-five minutes later.

Shortly thereafter, Press Secretary Kayleigh McEnany issued this statement on behalf of the White House: "Today, the President stood up for his Second Amendment rights and the rights of gun owners everywhere by standing his ground against an Antifa mob — controlled by Marxist agitators. Any suggestion that the President should apologize is absolutely mistaken and the President has no intention of doing so. If any apologies are necessary, they should instead come from the rioter who was shot by the President in self-defense."

That night on the cable news shows, coverage of the shooting was exhaustive:

Brian Williams on MSNBC reminded his audience of Trump's prediction on January

23, 2016 that "I could shoot someone on Fifth Avenue and not lose any voters."

On CNN, Anderson Cooper was speechless.

On CNN, Don Lemon said, "I think Trump has finally crossed the line."

On Fox News, Laura Ingraham commented: "If it was Obama who shot someone, the liberal media wouldn't have made a peep."

Rachel Maddow at MSNBC spent two segments on the shooting, then devoted the rest of that hour reminding viewers of the pandemic, the continuing and lethal spread of the virus that had now left over 300,000 Americans dead.

Back at the White House later that night, President Trump ran into Melania on his way to his indoor, room-sized golf simulator (installation fee $225,000).

"So, how was your trip to New York?" she asked sincerely.

* * *

CHAPTER 20

THE THIRD DEBATE — OCTOBER 22

The third and final debate between Biden and Trump took place at Belmont University — a private Christian university with ties to the Baptists — located in Nashville, Tennessee.

The first debate on September 29, moderated by Fox's Chris Wallace, was watched by around 73 million people, not all of whom managed to stay to the bitter end.

The second debate on October 15, at a performing arts center in Miami, drew 15% less viewers. Trump blamed Biden's low energy for the disappointing numbers.

Because of the continuing surge of the coronavirus, there was no audience at either event, and both candidates kept at least six feet apart at all times.

Both debates were followed by programs featuring fact checkers on CNN, MSNBC, and Fox. Combined, they counted over 135 partial misrepresentations, 96 misstatements of facts, and 474 outright lies. Most of those, as expected, were attributed to the President.

Anyone expecting a "knockout" blow from either candidate was disappointed. Though some pundits gave a slight edge to Trump in the second debate, primarily because for much of it, Biden either refused or forgot to take off his mask.

The third debate was moderated by NBC's Kristen Welker, known for her contentious questions to Trump as White House Correspondent.

Held in Belmont's empty 5,500-seat, multipurpose arena, this debate closely followed the first two: long, often unresponsive answers, vague generalities, and no real sparks between them.

Certainly nothing like the drama of the October 2016 second debate between Hillary and Trump, which took place right after the release of the *Hollywood Access* tapes where Trump was heard bragging how he liked to grab women by their pussies. To counter the fallout, Trump (at the suggestion of his then-Campaign Manager Steve Bannon) had placed Bill Clinton's female accusers (from harassment to rape) — Juanita Broadrick, Paula Jones, Kathleen Willey, and Kathy Shelton — in the front row of the audience, well within Hillary's line of sight.

Like its predecessors, the third debate between Trump and Biden droned on for eighty-five of its ninety minutes until Kristen Welker's last question to the candidates riveted those viewers who were still awake: "Can you both describe, as specifically as possible, your vision for the kind of America you would like to see at the end of the next four years?"

Biden went first:

BIDEN

I see hope for a better future. This
is not the first time our country has
been so divided and so challenged
by internal and external forces.
I remember the 1940s and the
Great Depression and the World
Wars in Europe and the Pacific. I
lived through the Sixties and the
racial injustices of the time and
the unpopular Vietnam War which
turned citizen against citizen,
fathers against sons. I was there in
2008 when the collapse of financial
institutions brought us to the brink
of insolvency, causing bankruptcies
and vast unemployment. But we got
through those times. And we can get
through them again.

But that will only happen if we are
governed by a strong and rational

leader — one who will fight this pandemic by listening to the medical experts — a leader who has a plan — a pathway for transformation. I am such a leader and I have such a plan. A plan to end racial injustices. A plan to give every American affordable health coverage. A plan to create jobs. To raise the federal minimum wage. To grant universal child care. To reduce the disparity of wealth between the super-rich and the rest of us. To allow easier access to college without burdening students with a lifetime of debt. To reduce the cost of prescription drugs. To make the systematic changes we need in this country — to make America the country — the country we all believe in — 'one nation, under God, with liberty and justice for all.'

At the end of my four years, I see the hope that we now have in our hearts transformed into a living reality. All it takes, as the great John Lewis once said, is that 'we keep the faith.'

Despite the fact that Biden was hardly specific or that his response was really a compilation of much of the same stuff he'd been saying in his stump speeches, it was one of Biden's better moments, at least, during the debates.

Now, all eyes and ears turned to Trump. Surprisingly, what followed was said in an even, measured tone without bombast, sarcasm, or ridicule. Nor did he veer off-topic, rambling on — as was his custom — about whatever popped into his head. Nor did he attack his rival or his enemies — the Deep State, the media, and the left-wing Socialists lurking around every corner. No, in fact, what followed was presented, in bullet-point fashion, with heartfelt — even precise — and, some would say, "Presidential" fashion:

PRESIDENT TRUMP

I see an America where Americans will not only land on Mars but be allowed back into Canada.

I see an America where the police can walk the streets without fear of being hurt.

I see an America where there is a monument to George Washington that actually looks like him.

I see an America where white businessmen have the same opportunities of black businessmen.

I see an America where neighbors will not be ridiculed for keeping their Christmas lights up all year.

I see an America where everybody will have health insurance that lets you pick your own doctor while keeping your underlying conditions.

I see an America where no one is allowed to sue a business or company just because they gave you the coronavirus.

I see an America where anyone who wants a ventilator can get a ventilator.

I see an America where Confederate flags no longer say 'Made in China'.

I see an America where the military are withdrawn from Iraq and stationed in Portland, Oregon.

I see an America where drinking a $1,000 bottle of imported wine is tax deductible.

I see an America where women who are harassed in the workplace are allowed to quit.

I see an America where little white boys and girls can go to school with

> little black boys and girls, even if their local school systems say it isn't safe.
>
> And I see an America where water comes out strong from faucets and showerheads, and toilets can be filled more than halfway.

Out of time, Kristen Welker thanked VP Biden and President Trump for a rousing exchange of ideas and bid a good night to the audience at home. If she had an opinion about anything she had just heard, she was not letting on.

* * *

CHAPTER 21

ELECTION NIGHT — NOVEMBER 3 AND 4, 2020 — MAR-A-LAGO

5:30 p.m.

The polls were still open on the East Coast as waiters from the Palm Room began to set up the dinner buffet: "Mr. Trump's Famous Wedge Salad" (half of a head of lettuce smeared in Roquefort dressing); an iced tower of seafood; beef tenderloin; seared sea bass; breasts of organic chicken; heirloom baby carrots; and the also-famous "Trump Chocolate Cake."

Ivanka and Jared had arrived earlier from New York to join family members and Trump's Senior Advisers in the family room at Mar-a-Lago: Eric and Laura; Don Jr. and Kimberly Guilfoyle (recovered from the coronavirus); and Hope Hicks (also recovered from COVID) — their eyes all trained on the walls of TVs.

As usual, Ivanka looked radiant, like she had just stepped off a cover of *Good Housekeeping* — with the cover line "Embracing Your Inner Diva" — wearing a pearl-white lace jumpsuit by Stella McCartney (retail $6,200). It was an outfit — discreet yet revealing — showing off a sculptured figure that confused even her best friends as to where Ivanka ended and cosmetic surgery began.

Jared — even in Palm Beach — wore his familiar dark suit, white shirt, and slim, dark tie — a costume appropriate for all occasions — whether it be a private meeting in Saudi Arabia with Crown Prince Mohammed bin Salman (net worth: a couple trillion dollars, more or less)... or a quiet prix fixe dinner at New York's Jean-Georges with Charles Packard, head of America's Wealth Management at Deutsche Bank (fined $150 million in July for its handling of the Jeffrey Epstein account)... or "davening" at Jerusalem's Western Wall with the Netanyahus.

Trump had retired to his bedroom to watch — without distraction — the returns alone, shuffling phone calls across the country to TV host Tucker Carlson, Campaign Manager Bill Stepien in Vegas, and Mike Lindell (inventor of MyPillow) in Minnesota.

Trump was especially concerned about Florida, which had him trailing Biden by four points, a state Trump had won in 2016 by a margin of +1.2. Governor DeSantis had called earlier to tell him that Florida was in the bag, but Trump knew by now that DeSantis was full of shit whatever it was he was talking about.

Stepien had already warned Trump that the numbers coming out of rural Polk County (Trump territory) might not be large enough to offset the Democratic counties around Miami and Miami Beach.

It came as a shock — with Florida still voting — that Frank Luntz on Fox News called the state for Biden. Outraged, Trump called the private number of Luntz's boss Rupert Murdoch to raise holy hell ("They shoulda fired the washed-up Luntz years ago" mumbled Trump to himself), only to have the call go right to voicemail.

Predicting Trump's pique, Hope Hicks popped in to tell Trump that Luntz, as usual, was way off base and her people were saying Florida remained in play. "It's still jump ball," she said, exiting quickly.

Meanwhile, in the Mar-a-Lago Grand Ballroom, supporters, mega donors, and campaign workers straggled in, anticipating Trump's victory party.

At one end was a platform stage with a gold lamé curtain and decorated with American flags. At the other, huge TV monitors, all tuned to Fox News. On each side of the stage, 35-foot screens showed snippets of the President in various poses: saluting the troops, meeting Heads of State, signing corporate tax cuts into law.

There were life-sized photo cutouts of Trump everywhere so you could have your picture taken with them. One woman — in

Trump regalia — mugged beside the replica with one hand on Trump's cardboard crotch.

The bar was open and more than a few of the early arrivals were surprised to find they had to pay $10 for a scotch and soda. Overhead, speakers blared with the infectious Trump theme song sung by the girls group "The Trump Gals."

THE TRUMP GALS

(singing)

AMERICA!
AMERICA!
LAND OF THE FREE
OH SAY THERE
CAN'T YOU SEE?

HOW IT'S GOT TO BE
PRESIDENT TRUMP IS HERE
FOR YOU AND ME!

AMERICA!
AMERICA!

LISTEN TO OUR SONG
FROM THE EAST COAST

TO THE WESTERN SHORE

HATERS OF LIBERTY
ALL BEWARE
WILL CRUSH YOU LIKE A BUG
WITHOUT A CARE
UNDER THE RUG!

AMERICA!
AMERICA!

GOD'S ON OUR SIDE
SO STEP ASIDE
OR YOU'LL END UP
WITH NO PLACE TO HIDE

AMERICA!
AMERICA!
AMERICA!

8:15 p.m.

Trump was now on his fifth Diet Coke. Pacing in front of the TVs, nothing he saw raised his spirits. He called Lewandowski in Virginia.

Lewandowski thought for a second about not taking the call. Finally, on the sixth ring, he picked up. “Yes, Mr. President,” he said tentatively.

“What’s it looking like?” asked Trump.

Lewandowski tried sounding as positive as possible. “We’re underperforming in the Southeast, but not by much and it doesn’t look like it’s a trend we can see nationally.”

Not exactly the good news Trump was hoping for.

“And Florida?”

“They’re still counting, sir. And they haven’t even begun on the mail-ins. Lots of votes left. Lots of hidden Trump voters, that’s for sure.”

Ever since 2016, that had been the theory: tens of thousands of hidden Trump voters — suspicious of the media and pollsters — who were reluctant to admit they were Trump supporters.

But if, in fact, Lewandowski believed that Florida was already lost, as was North

Carolina, he certainly wasn't going to be the one to break the bad news.

The New York Times, which had barely given Trump a 40% chance earlier in the evening, revised its figures downward, now giving Trump a 35% chance of winning.

And Chris Wallace — one of the few "objective" newsmen on Fox — was suggesting that, if present trends continued, Biden would become the 46th President of the United States. "That's if," said Wallace, backpedaling a bit.

Trump turned the sound up on MSNBC where Steve Kornacki was reviewing the first returns from the Rust Belt states — states that Trump had won in 2016 and would need to win again:

OHIO — Too close to call.

WISCONSIN — Biden held a slight lead.

PENNSYLVANIA — Tight, with Trump slightly leading, but votes from Philadelphia not in yet.

MICHIGAN — Biden doing better than expected in heavy African-American Wayne County. Not a good sign.

The Mar-a-Lago Grand Ballroom was now at full capacity with 1,000 supporters. Hopefully optimistic and fueled by more than one trip to the bar, they waved their tiny American flags and signs that read "Housewives for Trump," "Latinos for Trump," and "White People for Trump."

One of the wealthiest and most devoted donors — festively dressed in a star-spangled blue jacket, red-and-white striped tie, socks bearing Trump's image, and shoes with distinct messages: "Can't Trump This" on his right foot and "Build That Wall" on the left — danced with a woman in a designer dress featuring a sequined American flag to the canned music of the Mountain Boys' big hit "The Lord Is on His Way":

MOUNTAIN BOYS

(song over P.A.)

TIMES ARE DARK AND DREARY

OUR LIVES ARE ALL SO WEARY

AND THE EYES WE SEE FROM
ARE ALWAYS TEARY

SO BOW YOUR HEADS AND PRAY

THE LORD IS ON HIS WAY

CHRISTIANS ALL AWAKE

FREEDOM IS AT STAKE

LOOK UP INTO THE SKY
'CAUSE ANY TIME OF DAY

THE LORD IS ON HIS WAY

HEAR THE ANGELS SING

AS ALL THE DEAD ARISE

AND FLY INTO THE SKY
WHERE WE LIVE FOREVER

AND DEATH COMES TO US NEVER

THE LORD IS ON HIS WAY

IN THE NIGHT OR IN THE DAY

OH,THE LORD IS ON HIS WAY!

In spite of the air conditioning that was permanently set in Trump's bedroom at 69 degrees, there were traces of sweat forming on his nether lip, under his armpits, and between his thighs. He could feel himself begin to chafe. Tension furrowed his well-tanned brow. He sat hunched in front of the TVs, placing a call on his flip-top cell to Dr. Ben Carson in Detroit. Trump was hoping to hear that he'd been able to peel off enough African-American votes around Wayne County to carry Michigan as he had in 2016.

Candy, Ben Carson's wife, answered the phone. "Evening, Mr. President."

"I'd like to talk to Ben."

"I'm so sorry. He went to bed early."

"Wake him. It's important."

"He told me he didn't want to be disturbed. He has a headache."

Trump exploded: "A headache? I said I want to talk to him. I don't want to fuck him!"

"I'll have Ben call you right back," said Candy Carson evenly.

Trump threw his cell against the wall.

12:12 a.m., November 4

After Hope Hicks jumped off a conference call with Lewandowski, Bill Stepien, and their lieutenants, she reported the situation as it now stood to Jared, Don Jr., and Ivanka. The numbers in the Rust Belt states were looking, unfortunately, a lot like Florida. In a word, dismal.

From the electronically connected nerve centers in Vegas, Virginia, and Palm Beach, the data was the same: Trump was headed for a stomach-churning defeat.

Red states like Missouri, Utah, the Dakotas, Wyoming, and Montana were solid as expected. But Arizona was trending the wrong way and in Texas, surprisingly, Biden was still competitive. In Ohio, a state Trump had to win, Biden was polling stronger than expected.

On CNN, Don Lemon could barely contain his mirth as he reported that, as it was now going, Biden was headed for an Electoral College win of 325 to 215.

1:35 a.m., November 4

With 40% of the national votes yet to be counted, The Associated Press was the first to call the election for Joe Biden.

1:45 a.m., November 4

Trump appeared in the family room at his Mar-a-Lago's private residence in full fury. "They stole the fuckin' election," he roared, his face as bright red as his tie.

Shouting "Rigged! Rigged!" over and over, he grabbed at the Dungeness crab legs resting atop the cold seafood tower and threw them against the TVs, quickly followed by handfuls of his "Mr. Trump's Famous Wedge Salad" lettuce — chunks soaked in Roquefort dressing — along with one slice of his also famous Chocolate Cake, daintily lifted by its underlying paper doily.

No one in the room remembers him this out of control since Jeff Sessions had told him he was recusing himself from the Russian investigation and Reince Priebus and Sean

Spicer had to pry Trump's pudgy fingers from Sessions' 71-year-old throat.

Trump barked out his orders to Jared: "Call that Jew Sekulow and tell him I want every fuckin' lawyer he's got to file every goddamn lawsuit in the book."

To Hope Hicks: "You — get me Bill Barr. NOW!"

"You have his number on direct dial," she answered.

"I broke my fuckin' phone," screamed Trump.

Almost in tears, Hope Hicks searched her BlackBerry for the AG's number as Don Jr. and Kimberly Guilfoyle ran out of the room.

Somebody had to address the thousands of supporters waiting in the Grand Ballroom to hear from the President.

In 1985, when Trump turned Mar-a-Lago into a private club, he added what he called the

Donald J. Trump Grand Ballroom — 20,000 square feet that could hold a thousand guests. Influenced by Louis XIV's palace at Versailles, Trump spent at least $7 million on gold trimmings. Endless gilt-framed mirrors reflected endlessly its gold-and-crystal interior. The ballroom had been the sight of Don Jr.'s wedding to Vanessa Haydon in 2005 (she divorced him in 2018). And now it would fall on Don Jr. — in this same ballroom — to tell the remaining die-hard Trump loyalists exactly how things stood.

Kimberly Guilfoyle took the stage first to wild applause. She had changed into an Oscar de la Renta strapless, velvet mini-cocktail dress with a body-conscious silhouette (retail $4,999) to which she added a pair of especially designed star-spangled hip boots. She bounced to the mic and introduced her boyfriend Don Jr. (as "not only a hunk but a fearless fighter for liberty"), exhorting the crowd with whoops of enthusiasm so that, as Don Jr. joined her onstage in kisses and a warm embrace, he was met by cheers, applause, and slightly drunken chants of "USA! USA! USA!"

"Let me just say," he began, "that on behalf of my father — the President of the United States — thank you for your tireless and devoted support. Second, let me make this clear: what you've seen on television these last few hours has been Fake News. My father has not conceded. There are still many votes to be counted. And there are still many votes that have to be recounted. And my father will never give up until the real facts of this election are known to all Americans. So I say to you and to all those who are listening to me now — this is not the end of the election. This is just the beginning!"

With the crowd cheering wildly, Don Jr. and Kimberly exited arm in arm. Thousands of red, white, and blue balloons dropped from their nets hoisted high above the mirrored ceiling as, on cue, one of Trump's favorite songs blared from the sound system: Lil Smoke's "I Am Your King."

LIL SMOKE

(song over P.A.)

I AM YOUR KING

I AM YOUR KING

I AM YOUR KING

I AM YOUR KING

GOT ME A BRAND-NEW BENTLEY

DIAMONDS LIKE DOGS GOT FLEAS

AND I'M AS GODDAMN HARD AS TRIGONOMETRY

I AM YOUR KING

It had been prearranged between Hope Hicks and Biden's Director of Strategic Communications Kamau Mandela Marshall (former Obama speechwriter) that within an hour of the AP calling the election, the loser — in this case, Trump — was to call the winner and concede.

At 2:45 a.m. on November 4, Hope Hicks' phone rang. "Hope, it's Kamau. I was wondering why I hadn't heard from you."

Hope Hicks paused before replying: "We're not conceding."

There were at least fifteen seconds of silence before Kamau asked: "Why not?"

"There are a lot of votes that haven't been counted," she said.

"That could take weeks. All three networks say we've won — even Fox."

"The President has decided to wait and see."

"What states are you contesting?"

"The President has decided to wait and see," Hope Hicks repeated robotically.

"I'll tell the President-elect," said Kamau, getting in the last word.

* * *

CHAPTER 22

YET ANOTHER PHONE CALL FROM THE PRESIDENT TO THE AG

In the Barrs' sprawling mansion in McLean, Virginia, Christine Barr — after turning off the election returns — was sitting up watching a rerun of *Love Boat* on MeTV when her husband the Attorney General came in. He had just gotten off the phone with Trump.

"Now what's he want?" she said, muting the sound.

"He wants me to investigate the illegalities in the election."

"Every network says he lost."

"The President is convinced there was widespread voter fraud."

"And?"

"And he wants me to get the FBI to find the evidence."

"I suppose that's what you're going to do," said his wife.

"Well," said Barr, "I've always suspected there was something... problematic about mail-in voting."

"I thought it was a matter for the states."

"Not if I find widespread fraud. In that case, I certainly would have the right to seize all the ballots in question."

"But an investigation could take months."

"Possibly."

"And what happens to the country in the meantime?"

"The same thing that's been happening to the country for the last four years," said Barr.

"I shudder to think," said his wife.

"And now I'm going to see a man about a horse," he said, heading off to the toilet.

Christine Barr unmuted *Love Boat*. It was the episode in which Gavin MacLeod as the Captain fell overboard for a ditzy stowaway played by Charo.

* * *

CHAPTER 23

REACTIONS FROM REPUBLICAN SENATORS, PART 2

It was November 8 and President Trump remained defiant: The election was rigged and he was contesting every vote in every state he lost.

CBS White House Correspondent Paula Reid stood just south of the Rotunda in the Capitol Building — a few feet in front of the statue of Jefferson Davis — trying to get passing Republican Senators to comment on the President's refusal to admit defeat despite the Electoral College vote of 328 to 220 in Biden's favor.

MS. REID

(to lame-duck Senator Susan Collins:)

Senator Collins, would you care to comment on the President's statement

that he's not leaving the White
House?

SENATOR COLLINS

I'm sorry. I haven't heard his statement
as of yet and I never like to comment on
anything I haven't read personally.

(the Senator exits)

MS. REID

(to Senator Lindsey Graham:)

Senator, your reaction to President
Trump's refusal to concede the election?

SENATOR GRAHAM

I stand by the President in his
attempts to protect the voting rights
of every American.

(the Senator exits)

MS. REID

(to Senator Mitch McConnell:)

Senator McConnell, would you
care to —

SENATOR McCONNELL

I'm sorry. I'm late for lunch.

(the Senator exits)

* * *

CHAPTER 24

THE BUNKER

It was Friday, January 22, 2021, two days after Joe Biden was to have been sworn in as the 46th President of the United States. But Trump had not left the White House.

Protesters outside the White House had swollen in size and their numbers were now in the thousands, made up of all races and demographics, ordinary citizens who had come from every part of the country to protest Trump's refusal to concede an election they believed Biden had won fair and square.

With the arrival of pro-Trump defenders — armed militias, white nationalists bearing tiki torches, and motorcycle gangs from as far away as California — the Secret Service took action.

By 4:30 p.m. on Friday, Donald Trump, his immediate family — Melania, Ivanka, Jared, Don Jr., his girlfriend Kimberly

Guilfoyle — along with Vice President Mike Pence, his wife Karen, and AG William Barr — were ushered into the underground bunker beneath the East Wing of the White House. (Eric, his wife Laura, and everyone's children had been whisked to a safe location earlier that day.)

The bunker they were being herded into was officially known as the Presidential Emergency Operations Center (PEOC) and was built in the 1940s during World War II by Franklin D. Roosevelt and Harry Truman.

(In 2010, a $300 million excavation took place under the East Wing to update the water and sewage systems. The PEOC is manned — occupied or not — by around-the-clock joint military officers and noncommissioned officers.)

Trump and his gang were hustled single file past damp, water-stained walls, across broken tile floors, with pipes hanging overhead, and all kinds of undefinable mechanical equipment to, finally, a small conference room adjacent to the PEOC.

After the two Secret Service agents took everyone's dinner orders, a thick pair of steel doors closed behind them with a sharp, loud hiss, forming an airtight seal.

Left alone, they stood — almost frozen — stunned, fearful and uncertain as to what would happen next.

Unknown to Trump and his party, everything said and done after their arrival in the bunker was recorded by hidden cameras. The following is a transcript of that event:

The President: What a dump. *(looking around)* There are no TVs. Where the hell's the TVs?

Melania: Such a small space.

Ivanka: Maybe they gave us the wrong room.

The President: *(running his fingers across the table)* When's the last time anybody dusted in here? Christ — look at those drapes. Looks like something Obama picked out.

Seated, Barr makes notes on a yellow legal pad.

Karen: *(gasping)* Oh. Oh. Oh.

The President: What's the matter with her?

Pence: She's a bit claustrophobic. When she was a little girl, she got stuck on an elevator for six hours. They had to pull her up through a hole in the ceiling. *(consoling her)* It's all right, Mother. We're in a safe place now. Everything's going to be all right.

Kimberly: *(to the Pences)* You know, I just love the way you two are always holding hands. I only hope that Donald Jr. and I are as happy when we're your age. *(to Don Jr.)* Don't we, Pooh Bear?

Pence: That is so nice to hear. Isn't it, Mother?

Karen: *(to Kimberly)* I'm sorry. Who are you again?

Kimberly: Kimberly. Kimberly Guilfoyle. National Chair of the Trump Victory Finance Committee. Don Jr.'s fiancée. Well, not officially fiancée. *(pointedly towards Don Jr.)* Seeing as I still don't have that ring on my finger like I was promised.

Don Jr.: Please. Let's not start that again.

Karen: *(gasping)* Oh. Oh. Oh.

The President: Mike, get her to knock that off, okay? She's getting on my nerves.

Pence: Sorry, Mr. President. She'll feel better once she gets something to eat.

Kimberly: You can say that again. I'm starving. Haven't had a bite all day.

Ivanka: You'd think they'd at least have our salads by now.

The President: It wouldn't have taken so long if we all had cheeseburgers like I wanted.

Ivanka: Daddy, you know Jared and I can't mix milk and meat.

The President: Oh yeah, that.

Don Jr.: *(to Ivanka)* I don't know why. It's not like you're going to get sick or something.

Kimberly: *(trying to text)* My phone's not working.

Don Jr.: Because we're seven fuckin' stories underground, that's why.

Kimberly: You don't have to be so mean about it, Pooh Bear.

Don Jr.: I wasn't being mean. I was just pointing out that —

The President: *(interrupting)* Hey, knock it off, you two. You want to fight, go somewhere else.

Melania: *(to Kimberly)* Nobody asked you to come, you know. You could have gone with the others.

The President: Come on now...

Melania: *(sotto, sarcastic to Trump)* Oh, I'm sorry, I forgot how attractive you find her.

The President: *(protesting)* That was five years ago, for God's sakes.

Melania: *(sotto to Trump)* I can't believe you're paying her $15,000 a month and all she does is sleep with Don Jr.

The President: I'm not paying her. The campaign is paying her. Melania, please, I've got a lot going on right now.

After a pause:

Barr: *(looking up from his papers)* Mr. President, as I see the present situation, you have two options. The first option is this: Tomorrow night, you address the nation and tell the American people, in spite of the widespread voter fraud that at the moment appears to have cost you the election, you are willing to concede to Biden for the good of the country.

The President: The fuckin' election was rigged.

Barr: I know. I know. Just hear me out. *(beat)* The second option would be to address the nation and tell the American people that

you are invoking the Insurrection
Act of 1807 and, in addition, given
the widespread voter fraud and
civil unrest, you are also declaring
a national emergency whereby
you — as Chief Legal Officer under
Article II of the U.S. Constitution —
are therefore refusing to vacate
the Presidency until a complete
investigation of the election has
taken place by the Department of
Justice. *(pause)* Now I suggest we go
around the room and discuss the pros
and cons of the two options before
you make your decision. I have my
opinion, but I'm prepared to withhold
it for the time being.

The President: Ivanka, we'll start
with you.

Ivanka: Daddy, I think I speak for
Jared as well when I say we both
believe you've been a really terrific

President. But do you really want to do this for another four years?

Jared: Especially considering the way things are: 35% unemployment; food lines, miles long, in every city in the country; GDP down 6%; and a pandemic that's killed close to 400,000 Americans and is only getting worse.

Ivanka: So if you leave now, you can leave while you're still on top.

Jared: It's not like there aren't things you could do after.

Ivanka: Right. You could build that Trump Hotel in Moscow you always wanted.

Jared: Putin certainly owes you that much.

Ivanka: Or you could start your own TV network. The Trump Broadcasting System.

Jared: The Saudis already told me they'll invest billions.

The President: I know. But it's not the same as having your own army or Supreme Court.

Melania: My husband is no quitter.

Ivanka: You just don't want to lose that $50 million you get in your prenup.

Melania: Donald, are you going to let her talk to me that way?

Barr: I think it'll help everybody if we can keep this discussion as objective as possible. Mr. Vice President, what say you?

Pence: Mr. President, you've accomplished as much as any

President in American history. And I'm including Washington, Jefferson, and Ronald Reagan. I know I speak for the American people when I say how grateful we are for your years of dedication, hard work, and magnificent service. But politically speaking, I have to agree with Ivanka and Jared. This might be the best time to step aside.

The President: *(outraged)* Those sons of bitches steal the election from me and I'm supposed to quit? Well, the fuck I am!

Pence: You didn't let me finish. *(beat)* You're absolutely right and I want you to know that, on behalf of the American people, I stand behind you 100%.

A phone rings. Everyone looks around, puzzled as to its source.

The President: What's that ringing?

Jared: There's a red phone under the conference table.

The President: *(warily picks it up)* Hello... this is the President of the United States. Who is this? *(listens)* Hold on. *(holds phone out to Barr)* It's your wife.

Barr: *(taking phone)* Christine? How did you...? Yes, I'm in the bunker with the President. No, everything's fine. Nothing to worry about. Christine, I can't talk now, I'm in a meeting. I'll call you soon as I get out. What? Go ahead. *(writes on yellow legal pad)* Eggs, milk, and... dog food. Yes, I promise. Soon as I'm free. Love you too.

Barr hands the phone to President Trump, who hangs up.

The President: How did she know where to find you?

Barr: She called the FBI. Now where were we?

Don Jr.: Well, I say — no fuckin' way are we backing down now. Let 'em all eat shit!

Kimberly: That's telling 'em, Pooh Bear.

The door opens and two Staff Sergeant Marines, in full dress uniform (with medals and ribbons), enter, wheeling in two carts with dishes covered in silver domes.

Staff Sergeant #1: *(to President Trump)* Sorry, sir, it took so long. They're a little short-handed in the kitchen due to the coronavirus.

Staff Sergeant #2: *(holding up a plate)* Who had the Chicken Parmigiana made with grated Parmigiana-Reggiano cheese, flour with egg whites — no bread crumbs — sauteed in lemon butter?

Melania: That's me.

As plates are passed:

Staff Sergeant #2: Two Cobb salads — no bacon.

Ivanka: That's us.

Dishes are handed to Ivanka and Jared.

Staff Sergeant #2: One cheese and fruit plate, extra grapes.

Pence: That'd be for Karen. *(gives plate to Karen)* Here we are, Mother. Eat something, you'll feel better.

Staff Sergeant #2: Rack of lamb with rice pilaf.

Pence: That'd be me.

They pass the plates.

Staff Sergeant #2: Center-cut pork chop with mashed potatoes.

Barr: That's mine.

Staff Sergeant #2: New York steak, well done, side of fries. Extra ketchup.

The President: That's me.

Staff Sergeant #2: Chicken in the pot for two.

Ivanka: That's us again.

Staff Sergeant #2: Another steak well done.

Don Jr.: That's mine. Like father like son, eh, Pop?

Staff Sergeant #2: And one sushi combo.

Kimberly: That's for me.

Staff Sergeant #2: Sorry, they were all out of Spanish Mackerel.

Kimberly: Oh, that is a shame.

Staff Sergeant #1: And Parker House rolls for the table. Bottled water, pitcher of iced tea, three Diet Cokes, and one bottle of California Cabernet, 2016.

The President: Who ordered wine? I didn't order wine.

Kimberly: I ordered the wine.

Ivanka: You ordered red wine with sushi?

Don Jr.: *(to Kimberly)* Go easy on the wine, okay?

Kimberly: What's that supposed to mean?

Don Jr.: You know what that means.

Pence: Wait. I forgot to say a prayer before the meal.

Ivanka: Why do you always get to say the prayer?

Pence: *(hurt)* Fine. If you want someone else to say the...

Ivanka: *(interrupting)* Jared, why don't you say the prayer for a change?

Jared: Okay. Baruch atah Adonai, Eloheinu melech haolam, hamotzi lechem min ha-aretz.

Pence: In Jesus' name, amen.

Ivanka: You always have to sneak that in, don't you?

The President: Now can we eat?

Don Jr.: *(to Kimberly)* Pooh Bear, that's your second glass already.

Kimberly: *(downing the wine)* So? Who's counting?

Don Jr.: You know how you get when you have more than one.

Kimberly: Oh, really, and how do I get, if you don't mind me asking?

Don Jr.: All I'm saying is...

Kimberly: Pick. Pick. Pick. That's all you do. Why don't you just come right out and say it: I'm not good enough for you. Or your... family... *(begins to sob)* And after I raise millions for the campaign. After I catch the virus at that rally in Tulsa...

Karen: *(nibbling at her cheese plate, to Pence)* Poor dear, what's wrong with her?

Pence: Kimberly's just had a bit too much wine, that's all, Mother. Nothing to worry about.

Kimberly: *(throwing down her napkin)* Well, I'm sick of it. Sick. Sick. Sick. *(gets up)* Officer, could you direct me to the nearest powder room, please?

Staff Sergeant #1: Yes, ma'am. You go out here and in about a half a mile, you'll come to two tunnels. Take the one on the left, go past the emergency generator, and you'll see a door marked toilet. Make sure you don't take the tunnel on the right. That leads to a secret passageway under the Treasury Building.

Kimberly: Would you mind accompanying me... so I don't get lost?

Staff Sergeant #1: Not at all, ma'am.

Kimberly: Thank you so much. I have always depended on the kindness of strangers.

Don Jr.: Three glasses of wine and she gets this Southern accent.

Tipsy, Kimberly exits with Staff Sergeant #1 — arms linked.

Melania: You know why she was fired from Fox?

Barr: *(mouth full)* Can't say that I do.

Melania: Well, I heard she was texting pictures of her boyfriend's ding-dong to her co-workers.

Don Jr.: That's a lie! They only said that because they were jealous of her.

Melania: I'm only repeating what I heard, that's all. *(beat)* First she dates that awful Scaramucci person, now Don Jr.

Barr: Then it's agreed. The President will refuse to step down until the nation is assured that the election was not rigged against him. Am I right, Mr. President?

The President: Rigged. The whole fuckin' thing — rigged.

Barr: I suggest you address the nation tomorrow night to lay out your position.

The President: Jared, you write the speech.

Jared: It's still Shabbos.

The President: Fuck Shabbos, for Chrissakes. Never mind. I know what I have to say. And I'll give it from the Oval Office.

Barr: I'm not sure that's secure as of yet.

Ivanka: You know, Daddy, if you bring the Resolute desk down here, nobody'll know you're not in the Oval Office.

The President: Good idea. And bring down lots of flags for the background. And that little statue of Teddy Roosevelt on horseback. Nobody'll know the difference. *(pause)* And get Leo to do my lighting.

The red phone rings.

The President: *(picks up)* Hello? Hold on. *(to Barr)* It's your wife.

Barr: *(takes phone)* Yes, dear... *(listens)* Uh huh... uh huh. Really? You don't say?... Love you too.

Barr hangs up.

The President: What was that all about?

Barr: My wife says the news is reporting that the Virginia National Guard has started shooting rubber bullets at the protesters in Lafayette Park.

The President: Finally some good news.

Everyone continues to eat.

— End of Transcript —

* * *

CHAPTER 25

TRUMP'S ADDRESS TO THE NATION — JANUARY 23, 2021

PRESIDENT TRUMP

My fellow Americans. I come before
you tonight from the Oval Office
to inform you that, as of 6:00 p.m.
this evening, I have invoked the
Insurrection Act of 1807, which
empowers me — your one and only
President — to deploy the combined
powers of the U.S. military —
and what a beautiful military it
is — within these United States to
suppress the disorder, insurrection,
and rebellion now spreading
throughout our beloved nation.

It is the same Insurrection Act used by Presidents Thomas Jefferson, Dwight D. Eisenhower — a great, great general, couldn't have won World War II without him — and John F. Kennedy. So I'm in pretty good company, believe me.

(takes a drink)

I'm doing this because it's very simple. The rioters, the arsonists, the looters, the left-wing thugs now roaming our streets at will, destroying private property, public buildings — including police departments and religious institutions — must be forcibly removed from our cities.

(wipes his brow)

The destruction of our most precious historical monuments will no longer be accepted. First it was Robert E. Lee, then it was Andrew

Jackson — a great, great general, by the way. Couldn't have won the Civil War without him. And now we have these scum — because that's what they are — who want to tear down statues of Jesus Christ, who was born thousands of years ago and never even heard of the Civil War. Not going to happen. These radical, socialist organizations — including Antifa, Black Lives Matter, and Muslims for Biden, who burn our beautiful American flag, take a knee when they play our wonderful National Anthem, and attack our wonderful police who get hurt and never complain — will be apprehended and punished to the full extent of the law because I am your law-and-order President. Tonight, the nightmare ends and the American dream begins.

In addition, I have ordered our powerful Attorney General, and very highly respected, to authorize the FBI — sometimes they're great, sometimes not so much — to seize the ballots from all fifty states, including Washington, D.C. and the territories of Puerto Rico, the Virgin Islands, and Guam, to ensure a fair and accurate recount of this past November election. Which as we all know was one of the most corrupt elections in the history of this great country. We had voting machines that were made in China. We had mailmen robbed at gunpoint of their mail-in votes by some very bad people who then opened the ballots, forged names, and remailed the votes. Harvesting they call it. Everybody knows about it. Everybody knows it happened. Everybody knows the fraud connected to some millions and millions of mail-in votes. Those things are delivered by mail and

delivered into mailboxes and can
be taken out and nobody knows the
difference.

(straightens his tie)

This election, the Democrats have
had dogs voting. Cats voting. And
lots of dead people. That's right.
Thousands and thousands of mail-in
ballots with cemeteries as their
return address. Which is why,
until the Justice Department can
determine the rightful winner of the
Presidential election of 2020, I will
remain your one and only President.

(takes another drink)

For there is still much to do. There
is, above all, our economy. We had
a beautiful economy going in this
country. Some say it was the greatest
economy in the history of the world.
Then this scourge comes from China.
This virus. It's got a lot of names.

Some call it The Yellow Peril or the Kung-Flu. I call it my Jinx from the Chinks. I know you're going to say that's racist. No, it's not. It's a fact. Okay?

(pauses dramatically)

Like they said I was a racist when I closed down travel from China. Xenophobic they called me. But when I shut it down, that saved two, two-and-a-half million lives by doing that. Now, the Fake News, the crazy, lame-stream media, says that there are nearly 400,000 American deaths due to the China virus. One death is too many, but let me explain something to you. They lie, as usual. 25% of the deaths aren't even Americans. They're immigrants, migrant workers, illegal aliens, and people from poultry and pork processing plants. 60% of the deaths were old people. Who were going to die anyway. The sniffles would've killed these people they were so old and yet they call it coronavirus. Another 15% are cases that have been misdiagnosed. Some of you may not know what that is, but what that is — misdiagnosis — is people come into the hospital with a heart attack or dying of cancer and the doctors say, 'Oh, that's coronavirus' just to make me look bad. So that means in the country today, we really have zero deaths. Now, even zero deaths is one too many, but it means we're really doing a wonderful job. Our people are doing a wonderful job. Better than anywhere in the world, even South Korea, New Zealand, and Japan aren't doing a better job. But whatever the death rate — and even one death is too much — we have to open our economy. Have to do it. The cure can't be worse than the disease, okay? Because there's a lot more to life than living.

And that's why I'm still your President. I built the beautiful economy once and I will build it again. We had the lowest unemployment rate. The highest stock market in history. The lowest unemployment among African Americans since slavery. And we can — together — do it again. Together we can Make America Great Again! Because, my fellow Americans, the best is yet to come!

Thank you very much and good night.

* * *

CHAPTER 26

EPILOGUE — REACTIONS FROM REPUBLICAN SENATORS, PART 3

On January 24, 2021, *The Washington Post* reported that a light infantry battalion (known as "The Screaming Eagles") from the 101st Airborne Division, stationed at Fort Campbell, Kentucky, was on its way to Washington, D.C.

It was uncertain at the time of the reporting if this deployment was at the behest of President-Elect Joe Biden to forcibly remove Donald Trump from the White House or from still-President Donald Trump to clear protesters from Lafayette Park and surrounding neighborhoods.

Shortly after the story broke nationwide, CBS White House Correspondent Paula Reid stood just south of the Rotunda in the Capitol Building — a few feet in front of the statue of Jefferson Davis — trying to get passing Republican Senators' reactions to the recent developments:

MS. REID

(to lame-duck Senator Susan Collins:)

Senator Collins, can you comment on the story that the 101st Airborne is headed towards Washington?

SENATOR COLLINS

I'm sorry. I'm not familiar with the story and I never comment on stories I am not familiar with personally.

(the Senator exits)

MS. REID

(to Senator Lindsey Graham:)

Senator Graham, could you comment on the recent deployment of the 101st Division?

SENATOR GRAHAM

President Trump's campaign
promise was to 'drain the swamp'
and that includes the protesters now
threatening our nation's capital.

(the Senator exits)

MS. REID

(to Senator Mitch McConnell:)

Senator McConnell, would you
care to —

SENATOR McCONNELL

Sorry. I'm late for lunch.

(the Senator exits)

THE END

Ed. Weinberger, who has written for such diverse comedians as Bob Hope and Johnny Carson, began his career in the early '60s with Dick Gregory. He wrote and produced for *The Mary Tyler Moore Show* and co-created *Taxi, Dear John,* and *The Cosby Show*. He also executive produced and created *Amen, Sparks,* and *Good News*. Honors include three Golden Globe Awards, a Peabody, and nine Emmy Awards. In 2000, he received the Writer's Guild of America Lifetime Achievement Award. He is the author of the one-man play *A Man and His Prostate,* which starred Ed Asner and toured nationally for five years. In 2017, he co-authored the book *The Grouchy Historian: An Old-Time Lefty Defends Our Constitution Against Right-Wing Hypocrites and Nutjobs,* published by Simon & Schuster.